THE BOY
GAŻ

S.L. STERLING

The Boy Under the Gazebo

Copyright © 2021 by S.L. Sterling

ISBN: 978-1-989566-21-3

Paperback ISBN: 978-1-989566-27-5

Editor: Brandi Aquino, Editing Done Write

Cover Design: Joanna Walker

KENDALL

I slowly walked the aisles of the grocery store, my basket quickly filling with a pile of food no one should consume on a Friday night. Two bottles of wine, sweet-and-sour gummy bears, chocolate, because, well, it's chocolate, and a bottle of pop just in case. The only thing missing was something salty. It had been a long week, work had been stressful, and to top it off, my mother had been calling me non-stop, leaving message after message to find out if I was going home to this year's music festival in Bear Creek. I knew deep down that wasn't really the reason for her call, she knew very well that I was planning on going. She wanted to know who I'd be bringing with me as my date.

I was about to round the corner to the chip aisle when I felt my phone vibrate in my pocket. I pulled it out in time to see my mother's number on the screen. I rolled my eyes and quickly sent the message to voicemail, threw my phone down on top of my purse, and continued around the corner to the chip aisle. I stopped in front of my favorite brand and started looking over the bags for my favorite flavor when my phone rang again. Glancing at the screen, I picked up the phone and answered in an upbeat voice.

"Hey, Grayson!" It was a Friday night, and if I knew Grayson, which I did, he should be out on a date tonight, not calling me, which could only mean one thing—he had ended his relationship.

"Not much. What are you doing?"

"Just getting some snacks at the grocery store. What are you up to?"

"Not too much." The phone went silent as I waited for him to elaborate a little bit, but when he didn't, I became concerned.

"Are you okay? You're pretty quiet."

Grayson let out a huff. "Are you busy tonight? I was hoping maybe we could have a movie night?"

I smiled as Grayson stumbled over his words. He didn't need to say any more.

"So, I take it you finally broke up with Trish?"

Grayson let out a chuckle. "I guess you could say that."

"What was wrong with this one? Nail biter, bed hog, bad attitude?" I giggled.

"Oh man, where to begin. Let's just say her sarcasm wasn't really all that funny after a while. It was more hurtful towards people. Also, I found she wore too much makeup when we'd go out, and you know I can't stand that."

I'd known Grayson my entire life. We'd been best friends since we were six years old. When we were younger, we'd play in the playground and Grayson would push me as high as he could on the swing set. As we got older, we spend nights in his tree house playing board games. We never shared our first kiss, like many would think, and we didn't experiment with one another, nor were we friends with benefits like many people thought. Instead, he was one of the only constants in my life, which was a blessing, and I didn't mind not dating him, especially after I saw the reasons why he ended his relationships. I couldn't imagine how I, plain old Kendall, would ever be perfect under his microscope.

"Sure. See you around seven? Oh, and make sure you pick out a movie too. We'll make a whole night of it."

"Thanks, Kendall, you're a lifesaver."

I shook my head as I hung up the phone, grabbed the rest of the things I'd come for, and made my way back home. It was a little before seven when the buzzer rang. I quickly buzzed Grayson up and ran to the door as soon as I heard him knock.

"Hey, sweets, thanks for tonight." He wrapped his arm around my neck, pulling me in for a hug, just like he'd always done since we'd been kids.

"No problem. I already ordered the pizza, and we can flip for what movie we watch first if you want."

"What did you pick?"

"*Book Club*," I said with a smile on my face, preparing myself for the teasing I was sure was about to ensue. "What about you?"

"*The Shining*."

"Again?" I giggled. "We just watched that."

"Yes!" he said, giving me his puppy dog eyes. "Don't pick on me about my choices. I sit through every rom-com with you without complaint, and now you're going to make me watch a movie about four women reading *Fifty Shades of Grey*. Wasn't it bad enough that you told me all about those books when you read them."

"Man, it's a good thing you're cute, man." I giggled, slapping his cheek. "Come on."

Grayson kicked his shoes off and followed me into the living room, flopped down on the couch, and helped himself to a handful of chips from the bowl that sat on the table, just as the door buzzer went off.

"That will be the pizza. Here, make yourself useful and set up the movie would you," I said, throwing the remote onto his lap.

With half a pizza devoured, we sat at opposite ends of the couch, our legs commingled together watching the end of *The Shining* when the phone rang. I glanced at the call display and reached for the phone.

"Can you put this on pause. It's Mom," I said, tapping Grayson's leg. "Hey, Mom."

"Kendall, what are you doing home on a Friday night? I planned to leave a message."

I rolled my eyes. "Oh, you know, spending the evening with my couch and a pizza."

She'd been after me for months as to why I wasn't dating anyone, and I was pretty sure the last time she asked I gave her one of those sarcastic answers just to irritate her.

"Kendall, honey, you should be out with a nice boy," she chided. "I mean you are almost twenty-seven."

I looked at Grayson and rolled my eyes. He knew how badly these conversations with my mother bothered me. "What was it you wanted, Mother?" I asked, irritated that she was still going on about this.

"Well, your father and I were wondering if you were planning to come to Bear Creek with us next weekend for the USA Music Festival. We just need to know for numbers, and, of course, if you are planning on bringing anyone."

"Yes, Mom, I got your messages. I'll be there, and yes, put me down for a plus-one," I said, irritated, and without really thinking about the words that were flying from my mouth.

"A plus-one..." I heard my mother repeat, and then the line went silent. Had I rendered my mother speechless with my acknowledgment of an addition? "Who is it?"

I had no idea who I would take with me. There wasn't even the thought of a plus-one after I'd caught my ex with another woman, and now I had promised I would have someone materialized by the weekend. Instead of trying to laugh it off and backpedal, I blurted out the first person I thought of. "Grayson."

GRAYSON

At the sound of my name, I looked over to my best friend. I could see the shock and irritation line Kendall's face as she committed herself, and now apparently me, to whatever it was her mother had invited her to. She avoided my eyes and placed the phone on the table and buried her head in her hands. Then, running her fingers through her hair, her eyes finally met mine.

"So..."

"So what?" she asked, frustration lining her voice as she ran her fingers through her hair and scooted down farther on the couch.

"So, what did you just commit me to?" I asked, tapping the side of her leg, trying hard to get her to smile instead of panic.

Kendall buried her face in her hands again and

screamed. "Oh God, what have I just done?" she muttered probably more to herself than to me.

"I don't know. Why don't you tell me what you just did." I chuckled. I loved watching her squirm. I knew how her mother could be, and for some reason, it really bothered her that Kendall wasn't seeing anyone right now.

"I don't know what I did," she cried.

"I'd say you just appeased your mother." I chuckled lightly. "Do you secretly have a boyfriend you haven't told me about, that perhaps has the same name as mine and will be accompanying you next weekend?" I asked, grinning, ducking just in time to miss being hit in the head with a pillow.

"No." Kendall whimpered, shaking her head. "But I am going to have to find one fast I guess. Know anyone?"

"How fast?"

"Like Friday fast." She jutted out her bottom lip in a pout.

"Why, what is Friday?"

"It's that big music festival up in Bear Creek. You know how my parents always throw that huge summer party at the cottage during that festival." She rolled her eyes. "Mom's been on me about coming and asking me if I am bringing anyone. I want her off my case, and I just sort of snapped this time. I didn't want to hear it tonight. I guess I will just have to show up alone and tell them that I broke up with my plus-one."

I couldn't help but laugh out loud. She was way too

cute when she was annoyed. "Look, if it will help you and save you from humiliation, I can be your plus-one."

"Don't be silly. I am sure you have better things to do with your weekend than come with me and hang out with my parents."

"Not really. I have no plans for next weekend, and it sounds like you are in a bit of a bind. It might be fun."

"A bit of a bind, you think?" I watched as she twirled her hair around her finger over and over again, finally letting it go.

"I'm serious, Kendall. If it will help you out, I'll do it. I mean, I have to. I am apparently already going," I said, chuckling.

Kendall looked over at me, highly annoyed. "Sorry, you were the first person who came to mind. I guess you can say I sort of panicked."

"It's fine. I'll go with you or you'll end up in a much bigger bind. You know you'll never hear the end of it, especially if you don't show up with someone named Grayson."

"You have no idea."

"I remember how your mom can be. It's cool. We will go and listen to some awesome music, lay out under the stars. It will be great."

"I'm sorry I roped you into this."

"It's not a problem, trust me. We will pretend to be dating and it would be great to see your parents again."

Kendall looked at me and rolled her eyes. "Please, you

don't need to do this, and we don't need to pretend to be dating. I'll just tell them that we came as friends."

"Seriously, you want to tell your mother that and hear it all weekend. It's fine. Seriously, it will be fun. Might even teach your mom a lesson not to meddle. I'm up for it. A weekend away, good food, and it will get your mother off your back for at least the weekend. It's the least I can do for the girl who always drops whatever is going on to tend to my broken hearts."

Kendall dropped her head back and rested it on the arm of the couch, looking up at the ceiling. "I can't believe we are going to do this."

"Yep, we are, so get ready, baby. Let's have some fun. So when do we leave?"

"Next Friday, after work, and please don't call me baby."

"Okay, I will meet you after work on Friday. But I will need a pet name for you. What about doll or Kenny."

Kendall rolled her eyes at me. "I think I liked baby better."

"Perfect, it's settled. Baby it is. Now relax a little. We'll go and have a good time. You'll see."

A small smile settled on Kendall's lips and she looked over at me. "Thank you. You are a lifesaver, but if you want out, don't be afraid to tell me. I will totally understand."

"No way. You've saved my butt before. It's time I return the favor."

Kendall looked over at me, a little unsure of what she

might have just gotten herself into, and then smiled. "Now let's get back to our movies, shall we."

I hit play and shuffled down on the couch. I couldn't help but look over at my best friend—my beautiful, selfless best friend. I couldn't wait to spend this weekend with her.

Chapter 3

KENDALL

"Are you one hundred percent sure you still want to do this?" I questioned as I cradled my cell phone between my cheek and shoulder, while I folded the top of my lunch bag down. I'd spent most of the week worrying about the coming weekend. As much as I loved Grayson, I still was feeling bad about roping him into the weekend.

"For the thousandth time, yes. What are you so worried about?" Grayson asked, his deep voice pouring over the phone.

I blew out a breath. "Nothing. It's just, I know how my parents can be."

"Kendall, I can handle it. I deal with difficult people most of my day. Now what time did you say you wanted to leave?"

I knew that Grayson could handle it. I was just afraid

that he'd go over the top and my parents would end up loving him more than they already did. "I guess, say five."

"Yep, okay, fine. I will be by to pick you up then. I've got to get going."

"Wait, you're doing me the favor. How about I drive," I protested.

"No way. I want to make a good impression. Besides, what kind of boyfriend would I be if I allowed you to drive, baby." Grayson chuckled.

"Oh, my God. Okay stop," I said, laughing. "Fine, you can drive."

"All right, I can't have your parents hating me before they get to know me," Grayson said, matter of fact. I could already see the cocky grin on his face as he won the first battle.

"Would you stop, they already know you." I giggled.

"Sure, they know me, but not as your boyfriend. I can't just show up and be the same ole Grayson they already know."

I rolled my eyes, silently laughing to myself. "All right, listen, I've got to get back to work. See you Friday."

"Yep, see you Friday, baby."

I hung up my phone and shook my head at his last comment, then made my way back inside the hospital.

The remainder of the work week had flown by, and it was now Thursday night, and I was busy packing up my things for the weekend. I'd just gotten off the phone with Grayson, and now I stood in my bedroom looking down at my half-filled suitcase. I pulled out the two new bathing suits I'd just purchased for the trip, ripped the tags off, and threw them in my suitcase when the phone rang.

"Hello."

"So, who's the guy?"

My sister Jade was just as bad, if not worse than my mother. She'd tried to set me up with her fiancé's brother and a myriad of his friends two summers ago. When those guys didn't work, she proceeded to fix me up with just about every one of his co-workers, until I had finally gotten so fed up with her bad choices that I demanded she stop.

"I see you've talked to Mom," I said, rolling my eyes.

"I have, so spill it. Who is he? I had no idea you were even seeing anyone."

I bit the inside of my cheek, debating on if I should just tell her the truth straight up. "If you must know, it's Grayson."

Jade let out a loud scream of excitement, and I had to pull the phone away from my ear. "Finally, you guys are dating. I knew it would happen eventually. You guys were made for one another. I mean, the sexual tension between the two of you is insane and it's about time you acted on it."

I blew out a breath as I listened to my sister rattle on and on in excitement while I continued packing. When she finally ran out of words, I cleared my throat. "Listen, Jade, it's really not what you think."

"What isn't?" she questioned.

"Grayson and I, we aren't dating."

"Kendall, always the joker." My sister laughed. "If you're not dating then why would you say you were?"

"I'm not kidding. I never said we were dating. I said I was bringing him with me because I can't handle another event where you or Mom try to fix me up with someone. Seriously, the last time it was with the governor's son. I was so bored on that date I was ready to stab my eyes out with whatever blunt object I could find."

"Oh come on. The governor's son was gorgeous. He couldn't have been that bad."

"Yes, he was gorgeous, but he really was that bad, Jade."

"Yes, it must have been so hard to sit and stare at a six-foot-two hunk of muscle with gorgeous blue eyes."

I rolled my eyes and threw a light sweater into my suit-case. "Actually, it was painful because all he did all night was gloat about all the awards he'd won in the past six months. He also talked non-stop about some fundraiser he was doing in hopes that Dad would write him a huge check, and while he went on, I zoned out. I honestly couldn't even tell you what it was he was raising money for because I stopped listening to him after ten minutes."

"Okay, well, that is pretty bad. Perhaps he just wasn't your type."

"Not my type. Jade, please, of course they aren't my type. Then there was Mike, the son of that lawyer friend of theirs. It would have been more exciting to watch paint dry."

Jade laughed. "I'll give you that, he was pretty bad."

"And don't get me started with those idiots you tried to fix me up with. I'm pretty sure I read somewhere that one of them was arrested last week for beating some guy in a bar."

"Yeah, I saw that. It has been rather embarrassing for Rick down at the firm that he was even friends with John, so don't bring it up to him."

"I'm sure it has. I just don't want to hear about it all weekend and have Mom and Dad have one of their friends bring one of their sons out of pity. So Grayson volunteered. It will make Mom and Dad happy, and I will at least have a good time without all the unnecessary pressure."

"Well, it will be a pleasure to spend the weekend with you both, and perhaps by the end of the weekend you'll accept the fact that you are dating."

I couldn't help but roll my eyes. "Jade, please promise me that you won't mention this to Mom and Dad. I plan on just telling them that we didn't work out a few weeks after the weekend."

"Whatever you say, little sis. I won't say a word, not even to Grayson or Rick, I promise, but don't think for one second I'm not going to try and get you together for real."

I rolled my eyes. This was just like Jade. Always

meddling in things that she shouldn't. "Thanks, Jade. I have to go and finish packing. See you tomorrow."

"You bet. Have a good night."

I hung up the phone and pulled one of my favorite dresses from its hanger and folded it neatly and placed it on top of my suitcase, then grabbed a towel and made my way to the bathroom to shower. I just hoped that Jade could keep her mouth shut long enough to allow me one weekend of peace.

Chapter 4

GRAYSON

I'd finished my last shift at the hospital early this morning and had slept for a few hours before packing my bags and heading to the coffee shop. I'd grabbed us each a coffee for the drive and some muffins. The aroma of fresh coffee filled the cab of my truck as I pulled into the parking lot of Kendall's building. I was about to pull into a parking spot when I spotted her over by her car, suitcase in hand.

"All right, let's get this show on the road," I said as I hopped out of the truck. I reached down and took her bag and threw it into the back of my truck. "You have a map?" I asked.

"Yep." She held a folded map up for me to see as she climbed into the passenger's seat.

It only took me a minute to get us onto the highway, and once we had a little bit of road behind us, I leaned over and turned the radio down.

"Hey, that's a good song," Kendall said, looking up from the map as she was trying to determine which way would be the best way for us to go in order to avoid traffic.

"I know, but I think it's time we get our story straight. You know, who does what for work, any conversations we should avoid, how long we've been dating, how serious we are. It's been a long time since I've seen your parents, so it's whatever you want. You're the one in control here."

Kendall looked over at me as if to question if I were feeling okay, and then smiled. "Our story?"

"Yes, our story. If we don't get on the same page now, it won't be believable that we are together," I answered. "I'm sure that the last thing you will want is the whole entire story falling apart in front of your parents."

I watched as she took what I was saying into consideration, and then she nodded. "Okay. You are probably right," she said, blowing out a breath. "All right, for work, there's really no need to change anything there. You'll be starting your internship at the hospital in a couple of months, I am sure it will impress both my mother and father to think I'm dating a soon-to-be doctor."

"Okay, how long have we been together?"

I watched as Kendall bit her bottom lip in thought and I smiled to myself. She was so cute when she was trying to figure things out.

"Um let's say eight months."

"Eight months? I thought your mom just set you up on

a date not seven months ago. Are you cheating on me already?"

Kendall rolled her eyes at me. "She tried, but I canceled that date last-minute, so it would make sense."

"All right, eight months it is. How serious are we?"

"I don't know. How serious do you want to be?" She giggled, twirling her hair around her finger, a slight blush on her cheeks.

"Where will I be sleeping?" I asked, looking over at her and raising my eyebrows.

Kendall broke out laughing and smacked my arm.

"What? I'm only asking. I mean, I may or may not have packed pajamas."

"Ugh, you're impossible. They don't need to know how serious we are. It's none of their business." Kendall shrugged. "Anyways, topics to avoid: whatever you do, don't bring up politics with my dad. Don't comment on anything he says. Just do yourself a favor and agree, even if you disagree with every fiber of your being."

"Noted." I turned onto the road leading up to Bear Creek and slipped my hand into Kendall's. She looked down at our hands and over to me. "What are you doing?"

"Practicing."

"Practicing what?"

"Holding hands. I think it's important we get used to doing this."

"Whatever you say," she whispered, then relaxed back into the seat and blew out a breath. "Whatever you say."

An hour later, music blaring, we finally pulled into the driveway of her family's mountain cottage and cut the engine. I hopped out of the truck, while Kendall gathered up the wrappers from our dinner and threw them into the fast food bag. I walked around the truck and opened her door, holding my hand for her to take.

"I see your laying it on pretty thick already."

I smiled as she slid out of the truck, her eyes meeting mine the entire time. "Hey, if we are going to do this, we need to be convincing, right? Besides, what would your parents think if they looked out the window and I wasn't being a gentleman," I whispered, leaning in and kissing her on the cheek.

"Please." Kendall giggled, rolling her eyes at me as I stepped away from her. I pulled our bags from the back seat, and together we walked hand in hand to the front door.

Kendall raised her hand and knocked on the front door and together we waited. I placed my hand on her lower back, and she jumped just as the door opened. I quickly pulled her into me and surprised her by placing a kiss on her lips.

"Kendall, Grayson, so glad you're finally here," Kendall's Mom greeted us. "Come on in. I'll show you to your room, then you can come up and meet everyone," she said, stepping aside. I walked in first, and she wrapped her arms around me and gave me a big hug. She wasted no time as she directed us down a set of stairs to the basement. She stopped right at the bottom of the stairs and opened a door to one of the spare bedrooms. "This is where both of you will stay. I was going to put you upstairs, but Jade and Rick took that room."

I could barely contain my laughter at the look on Kendall's face as we both stepped into the room and looked around. A king-sized bed sat in the middle of the room, and we both glanced to one another.

"Will this be okay, Kendall. It's the only spare room left with a king bed, except the guest house, but that is being occupied for the weekend by the organizer of the music festival."

When Kendall didn't immediately respond, I turned to her mom. "It will be fine. If you can give us a few minutes to get settled, we will be right up."

"Sounds good. I hope you are both hungry. We have a lot of food."

"We are starved," I said, smiling, even though it was the furthest thing from the truth.

"All right, you two, get settled. We will see you upstairs," she said, closing the door and giving us our privacy.

Immediately, I turned to Kendall. She stood staring at the bed in the center of the room and then turned to me, a look of apology on her face.

"How is this going to do?" she said, gesturing to the bed.

"It will be fine. I'll just sleep on the floor. It's not a big deal," I said, resting my hands on her upper arms.

"No, I will. You're doing me the favor and besides I used to sleep on the floor when I was a kid," Kendall said, shaking her head.

"No, you won't. It's fine, really."

"Really. Just relax and go with the flow okay," I said, pulling her into me for a hug.

She wrapped her arms around me and buried her face in my chest. "I'm so sorry I dragged you into this," she mumbled.

"I said it was fine. I'm not upset."

I couldn't help but hug her tighter as she tightened her embrace on me and I placed a kiss on the top of her head. "We should get ready and get upstairs."

Chapter 5

KENDALL

While Grayson took a few minutes to himself to relax after the drive, I busied myself in the washroom getting ready for dinner. I walked into the bedroom to see Grayson going through his suitcase. I had quickly showered and changed into my favorite halter-style summer dress and placed my toiletry bag on the nightstand.

"I was just going to hop in the shower," Grayson said, looking over his shoulder at me. When his eyes landed on me, he stopped what he was doing and stared.

"What? What is it?" I questioned, looking down at myself, fearing I had something embarrassing stuck to me, like a pair of panties.

Grayson shook his head and turned back to his suitcase, pulling out clean clothes. "Nothing at all. I'll be up shortly."

I frowned as his eyes met mine as he walked past me. Once he was gone, I took another look at myself in the mirror, still worried that he wasn't telling me something. When I found nothing, I looked in the direction he had gone and shook my head. He seemed to be acting strange. He'd seen me in this dress many times before. I shrugged it off and made my way upstairs.

"Hey, honey, did you want to start cutting up those vegetables for the tray, please," Mom asked as I walked into the kitchen. Guests would be arriving shortly, and it looked like she was falling behind on a few things.

"Sure." I grabbed an apron from the pantry and slipped it over my head. I was just about to start cutting up a head of cauliflower when Mom turned to me.

"So, Grayson seems nice. How long have you two been seeing one another?"

"About eight months, and Mom don't act like you don't know him."

"Oh. Is that why you didn't go on the date with that young fellow I set you up with?"

I closed my eyes as the knife sliced easily through the cauliflower. "Yes."

"Well, honey, why on earth didn't you just tell me."

Jade came walking into the kitchen and sat down on one of the breakfast stools, throwing a piece of broccoli in her mouth. "Yeah, Kendall, why didn't you just tell her," she mocked, giving me a smile.

"Kendall?"

"I don't know, Mom. I guess because we had just started seeing one another and I didn't want to start sharing it with the entire world."

"Kendall, I'm your mother."

"I know," I said, forcefully chopping a carrot in half.

"If you know then why wouldn't you tell me? It's been so long since I've seen him. What does he do?"

"He will be starting his internship at the hospital in a couple of weeks."

"A doctor! Impressive. So is it serious between the two of you?" Mom questioned.

I gripped the handle of the knife hard enough that my knuckles turned white and looked to my sister who sat there smiling at me, waiting for my response. I swear she loved the fact that Mom hounded me this way.

"Yeah, just how serious is it, Kendall," she prodded.

"It's been eight months, Mom," I answered, swallowing hard. I felt like a wild animal caught in a trap. I didn't really know how to answer her, and that was when Grayson appeared in the kitchen. It was like he had heard the entire conversation from the stairs and wasted no time. He walked around the island and placed his hand on my lower back, leaned in, and kissed my cheek. "I'm just going to go out on the back deck for a bit. Did you need anything?" he asked gently, squeezing my side.

I looked him directly in the eye and shook my head.

"I'm good. Thanks for checking," I answered through clenched teeth.

Grayson smiled at me. "Okay, baby, you need anything at all, you just come out and get me," he said, winking at me.

I felt as if I were on fire as I watched as Grayson made his way out the back door to where Jade's fiancé was talking with Dad.

I looked over to Mom who seemed to be at a loss for words as she had watched our exchange. I went back to cutting up the vegetables, while Jade walked around to help Mom with platting deserts.

I had just plated the last little bit of vegetables when the doorbell rang.

"Jade, honey, can you get that please," Mom asked. "Kendall, put these out on the table over there," she said, signaling to plates of appetizers.

I wiped my hands on my apron, untied the back, and pulled it over my head. I looked out the back window and caught Grayson watching me. I smiled in his direction, but he didn't acknowledge me. He just continued watching me and sipping on his beer then turned his attention back to Jade's fiancé, nodding in response to whatever was being said.

I carried the plates of appetizers over to the large table Mom had set up, organizing everything neatly, and then I looked over to where Grayson stood. I was lost in my own private thoughts when I felt a tap on my shoulder and turned to see my mother staring at me. "I need help with the desserts too."

I tore my gaze away from Grayson and followed her over to the kitchen where I picked up two more plates and carried them back over to the table.

Chapter 6

GRAYSON

I had never been so glad to step out onto the back patio, the cool summer air hitting my face. Kendall's father and Jade's fiancé Rick were standing off to the side engaged in a heated debate. They both looked my way and continued whatever they had been talking about as if I weren't even there.

Instead of approaching them, I walked over to the edge of the patio and looked out over the yard. I hadn't expected my body's reaction when I had leaned in to kiss Kendall on the cheek. The scent of her perfume combined with the scent of her had sent my body into overdrive. I'd always been attracted to her but was never sure of how to make the first move. I had always been so confident with every woman I had been with, but when it came to her, she paralyzed me. I needed to get a grip on myself because this was my only chance. I planned to take this entire weekend to make her see exactly how I felt about her. I blew out a breath and made my way over to the other two men.

"Like I said, Rick, you have no clue what you're talking about," Kendall's father said, stepping into the house for a minute.

I looked at Rick, who nodded and lifted his beer, tilting it toward me.

"How's it going?" he asked.

"All right. You must be Jade's fiancé," I said, holding my hand out for him to shake.

"Rick, and you must be here with Kendall."

I nodded as we both shook hands. Rick turned and pulled another beer from the fridge, holding it out for me to take.

"Thanks," I said and placed my empty bottle on a table with others.

"How long have you two been dating?"

I was about to answer when Kendall's father came back outside, ignoring me, and jumped right back into the conversation he had been having with Rick. I tried without much success to join in, but he just kept taking over the conversation.

I glanced inside the house and watched as Kendall stood there cutting vegetables. She was absolutely gorgeous, her softly tanned skin accentuated by the bright colors of her dress. Her soft brown hair was pulled back in a ponytail, and she had pulled it to the side, where it lay gently on her right shoulder. I couldn't help but allow my eyes to wash over her body as she turned away from where she had been standing to grab a different vegetable peeler. The dress she wore clung to the soft curves of her body, and I wondered what it would be like to actually be able to touch her the way I had wanted to. I was so wrapped up in my thoughts it took me a minute to realize she was now looking my way with a confused look on her face, which quickly turned into a soft smile.

"Grayson, you have to admit the mayor is doing a bad job, except in the health field," Rick said, hitting me in the arm.

I glanced to both Rick and Kendall's father, who stood there waiting for me to respond, and then I remembered what Kendall had said in the truck about politics and her father. I tried hard to remember what they had been saying during their conversation and what her father had said so I could side with her Dad, but I had been so lost in thought watching Kendall I hadn't heard a word they had been saying.

"Rick, don't be ridiculous. They didn't need to open such a big unit for cardiac care."

I took a swig of my beer. There was no way I could side with this man on this topic. I had spent all this time in school and was now getting ready to spend the next four to five years doing my residency as a heart surgeon.

"Actually, sir, I disagree. The hospital's current status

before was not fit to care for the amount of heart patients they had. They actually did need to build that unit."

Kendall's father looked at me and scoffed. "What would you know about it," he questioned, looking me up and down.

"I know because I am starting my residency at the hospital. They have needed that cardiac unit for the past four years, and I am glad that they it's finally built and that they are properly investing into it."

Kendall's father looked at me, shook his head, and then turned his conversation back to Rick. I stepped off to the side and once again looked out over the property. I could tell I had blown it.

"Hey, Grayson." I turned to see Kendall's sister Jade standing there with another beer. "Want a beer?"

"No thanks, I'm good," I said, holding up the one I hadn't even begun to finish.

"Been cast aside I see," she said, nodding over to where Rick and her father stood.

"Yep." I smiled.

Jade was about to ask me something when I noticed Kendall standing in the doorway, a look of unease on her face.

"Hey, babe," I said, smiling, and walked over to her, taking her hand. She walked over with me and stood at my side.

Jade looked at us both and then excused herself, going

over to stand with Rick. I looked down into Kendall's eyes and smiled. "What is it?" I questioned.

"Get ready. People are here," she whispered.

"I'm ready. Are you." I chuckled as she shook her head.

A few minutes later, we stood mixed with the rest of the guests. Each of them, in turn, asking us the same questions we'd been bombarded with since we'd arrived. How long we'd dated, how we met, and numerous other questions that neither of us had been prepared for. Yet the longer we stood together, the quicker the answers came, and we each took turns answering, neither of us slipping up.

Chapter 7

KENDALL

"Well, it's pretty much settled. Your father hates me already," Grayson said coming, into the kitchen and sitting down at the breakfast bar.

I finished drying the last serving tray, folded up the dishtowel, and hung it over the towel rack. "I told you on our way up here to just agree with whatever he said," I said, laughing, turning and filling up his glass with the last of the juice punch.

"Kendall, there was no way I could agree. It goes against everything I stand for. You know it and you should agree with me. You've seen it too. I can't believe that the man would actually say that the hospital doesn't need the additional funding for the cardiac unit."

"There is absolutely no reasoning with my father, Grayson, especially when his mind is made up. It doesn't matter."

Grayson looked at me and shook his head. "Well, so far, as your fake boyfriend, I am not racking up the points, that much I'm sure."

I let out a laugh. "It's okay. You're stacking points with me. This is the first time I have been able to be around my mother in the last three years without being harassed about whom I'm dating. Even though it started out rocky."

I watched as Grayson drank down the last of the punch in his glass and then looked around the kitchen. "Did I hear you say good night to everyone?"

"Yep. Jade and Rick turned in shortly after Mom and Dad. I told them I would finish up down here."

Grayson looked around again and then over to me, a sly smile on his face.

"What?" I asked with a giggle in my voice.

"Feel like going for a dip?" he asked, raising his eyebrows. "It's beautiful out."

"As long as we are quiet, sure," I answered, looking around to make sure I had done everything my mother had asked of me.

Grayson looked over at me and grinned. "I'm gonna go get changed."

Ten minutes later, I emerged onto the back deck, wrapped in a towel, to find Grayson already in the pool. He was floating on his back with his eyes closed. As I approached the edge, I couldn't help but check out his muscular chest and tight abs. I wondered what it would be like to be wrapped up in his arms or to be able to run my hand over him. I was so focused on those tight abs that I didn't notice he had opened his eyes and lay there watching me.

"You getting in, or are you going to stand there watching me?" he questioned.

I jumped at the sound of his voice and pushed those thoughts of him from my mind, but I could still feel the heat rising to my cheeks at the fact I'd been caught staring at him.

"I'm coming," I said, holding onto the towel that was wrapped tightly around me like it was my lifeline.

"Are you going to swim in that towel?" He chuckled as he stood up and dipped his head under the water.

While he was under the water, I dropped the towel quickly, revealing my bikini-clad body, and climbed into the water. I had no idea why I was so uneasy and embarrassed about my choice of bathing suit. Grayson and I had gone swimming together plenty of times. He'd seen me in every bathing suit I owned, some much more revealing than the one I was wearing right now. I swam to the far end of the pool away from Grayson and popped my head up above the water's surface. I leaned up against the wall of the pool and watched as Grayson began swimming toward me.

A funny feeling in the pit of my stomach started to rise as he swam closer, finally coming up in front of me and placing his hands on the pool's edge on either side of my body. "So, how did you feel about tonight? I think we worked well together. Think we were believable and pulled it off?" he asked, looking into my eyes.

I shrugged. "I don't know. We did work well together as a team."

When I looked up and met Grayson's eyes, I was surprised to find he was looking at me in a way he never had before, and silence fell between us. My eyes flew from his eyes to his lips, and, for a moment, I wondered what it would be like to kiss him. The more the thought ran through my mind, the more I was finding it hard to breathe.

"What's on your mind, Kendall?" I could feel the puff of Grayson's breath as he spoke, and it sent a surge of electricity through me.

I swallowed hard and cut eye contact with him. "It's just, um...it's getting late. We should probably head inside," I whispered.

He didn't say anything, just continued looking at me, and then he nodded and backed away slowly. As he swam to the other end of the pool, I wanted to scream at him to come back. I wanted to scream at him to kiss me, but I knew that I was being stupid. Grayson had never indicated he felt any way about me other than friends. I shoved down the feelings I was having and slowly followed, climbing out of the pool and wrapping my towel tightly around me.

Chapter 8

GRAYSON

An hour later, I was still wide awake, lying on the floor, my arms crossed behind my head, staring up at the ceiling. Kendall had fallen asleep almost as soon as her head hit the pillow, but I hadn't been able to shut my mind off.

I'd given my current relationship status a lot of thought over the past five months. I'd dated ten girls in that short time, each and every one of them ending on my call and for some stupid reason, then I'd realized it was because none of them could ever compare to Kendall. She had such a natural beauty, not only in looks but in personality.

We had always been friends, and over the years, my crush on her would come and go like waves in the ocean. That was why I never acted on it. I knew that if I made a move too soon, she would be gone out of my life forever, and that was something I wasn't willing to risk. She was the kind of girl who needed to take a relationship slow and one who always had to be sure of herself. She never dove into anything blindly like I did. She'd had bad experiences with all the guys she'd dated, only because they never realized the truth—that she was a forever girl in the truest sense and not one who was just looking for a one-night stand.

She was sweet and snuggly, silly with a side of snark, smart and intelligent. I actually thought we would be perfect together, but that only became obvious after a breakup, so, in order to avoid making a food of myself, I would always make sure I had a steady stream of dates booked afterward. However, this past week I hadn't had a single date. Not because no one was available, but because I knew in my heart she was the one.

I had so badly wanted to kiss her out in that pool but just couldn't bring myself to do it. I knew she had no idea how I felt about her, and I didn't want to scare her away. With Kendall I needed to calm down and take my time, so when the opportunity to spend a weekend with her arose, I wasn't going to back out. I had one weekend to make her see—see me differently, see us differently—and I was going to do whatever it took to make it happen. I was going to start bright and early tomorrow morning.

KENDALL WAS STILL CURLED up in the blankets sound asleep when I woke. It was only seven, and I took my time to shower, get dressed, and make my way upstairs without waking her.

"Good morning, Grayson," Kendall's mom, Jean, greeted me.

"Morning. I was wondering, would it be okay if I cooked breakfast this morning for Kendall and I?"

"Oh that is lovely," she said, smiling as she looked around her clean kitchen. "Of course, we are just on our way out with Jade and Rick to head down to the music festival. Should we save you a spot?"

"Yes, please do, and please don't worry. The kitchen will look the same once I'm finished."

"All right, you should find everything you need in the fridge or pantry there," she said, heading toward the front door.

Once I said good-bye to everyone, I made my way to the kitchen and began looking for a bowl so I could get breakfast going.

I'd been working away for almost thirty minutes and had just flipped the last of the bacon out of the pan and poured the batter for two large pancakes onto the griddle when Kendall came around the corner. She looked gorgeous in a black halter top and low-cut jean shorts. It was all I could do not to stare, and quickly busied myself. "Good morning. Take a seat. I will get you some juice," I said, heading over to the fridge and pulling out the orange juice.

"What are you doing?" she questioned, and looked around the kitchen, implying I had lost my mind.

"What's it look like I'm doing. I'm making us breakfast!" I answered, quickly flipping over the pancakes before they burned, and smiled at her.

"Dude, you drink coffee for breakfast," she said, a weirded-out expression on her face as she sat down at one of the place settings at the breakfast bar. "Are you feeling okay?"

"Yes, I'm fine." I didn't pay any attention to her reaction. I just grabbed the pitcher of juice and filled both our glasses.

"Where is everyone?" she asked, looking around.

"They've already left for the festival. They are going to save us a spot. I figured after we eat we can head down and join them, unless, of course, you wanted to do something else first," I said as I flipped the pancakes onto our plates, divided the bacon, and slid Kendall her plate.

"That sounds fine. Although, there is one thing I would like."

"What would that be?"

"I'd really like it if you stopped being weird. You're freaking me out."

I made my way around the breakfast bar, but before I took a seat, I leaned in and kissed her on the cheek. "Whatever you say."

THE HOT AFTERNOON sun beamed down on us as we lay on a blanket listening to the current band that was on stage. Kendall had been oddly quiet since we had arrived, and I was afraid it had something to do with this morning. She'd barely even looked at me after we'd arrived. A couple of hours into the morning, Jade and Rick had invited us to go with them over to another stage and watch a band. At the same time that I said yes, Kendall declined, insisting she just wanted to lie in the sun and listen to the music here, but she insisted that I go with them. I was about to get up and go when one look from her father made my choice for me, so here we were, sitting with her parents.

I was propped up on my arm, watching the band on the stage, when Kendall rolled over onto her stomach and turned her head to face me. She looked up at me and softly smiled. "Would you be able to put some sunscreen on my back? I feel like I might be getting burnt," she questioned as she raised herself up on her elbows. I averted my eyes from her perfect bathing suit-covered breasts and watched as she pulled out the tube of sunscreen from the bag she had carefully packed and handed it to me.

"Lay down," I whispered as I sat up and shook the tube, squeezing some lotion into my hand. I rubbed my hands together and then started at Kendall's shoulders, carefully beginning to rub in the lotion. Out of the corner of my eye, I could see her father watching my every move, especially as I spread the lotion around the warm skin of her lower back, making sure that it was completely absorbed before I stopped. I was just about to put the lotion away when she whispered, "Could you do the backs of my legs too."

I felt my cock jump at the thought of being able to have my hands on her a little longer when I caught her father looking directly at me. It was like he could read my mind, but instead of sitting there looking guilty, I smiled in his direction and then leaned down close to Kendall and whispered, "You'll have to do them. Your father looks like he is ready to kill me," I said, kissing her cheek. "Want something to drink?"

"Water would be good."

I placed the tube of lotion down beside Kendall and sat up. "I'm going to get some drinks. Anyone want anything?"

"We're good," Kendall's father barked, finally turning his attention back to the stage.

"Daddy, be nice." Kendall sighed, sitting up and grabbing the sunscreen.

I winked at her and wandered off in the direction of a drink vendor and purchased two bottles of water, then made my way back. I had just dropped the bottles of water on the blanket between Kendall and me when her father returned from the bathroom.

"Ryan, are you all right?" Jean questioned, alarm filling her voice.

I looked up and noticed the pale look of his skin. His breathing seemed a little labored, and he was sweating.

"Dad, are you okay?" Kendall asked, standing up and walking over to him.

"I'm fine. I'm fine. Get away from me," he said, shoving her away when she went to help him sit down.

"No, Dad, maybe you should have Grayson check you over."

"I don't need anyone checking me over, especially some kid. I'm fine," he barked.

"Sir, with all due respect, I think perhaps you should get out of the heat, get into some shade for a while, and call your doctor."

"What the hell would you know," he scoffed.

"No, Ryan, I think the kids are right. Perhaps a call to Dr. Shiff wouldn't be a bad thing. This is the second time you've had this happen in the past couple of months. It's almost four anyways. Perhaps we should head home. You can lie down and I can get dinner ready."

"Fine, if it will make you all stop harping on me, we'll go, but we are not calling the doctor. I'm perfectly fine."

We walked back to the parking lot with Ryan and Jean, and then we made our way over to a different stage. I spread the blanket out over the ground and sat down first, leaning back on my arms. Kendall surprised me by crawling between my legs, leaning back on me, and using me as support.

"You okay?" I asked, wrapping my arms around her.

"I'll be okay. I'm just worried about my dad. He didn't look very good, and he's so stubborn. I know my mom had mentioned something, but I didn't think anything of it until now."

"Well, hopefully, your mom will get him in to see his doctor. That's all you can hope for. Now, let's just relax for a bit, and then we will head back to the house, okay."

Kendall nodded and relaxed into me, and together we sat listening to the music that was playing.

KENDALL

Grayson had always been my rock. I had been so shaken at seeing my dad not feeling well that I hadn't realized just how happy I was to have Grayson here with me. I really did need him, and he had done what he needed to do to comfort me. He held me in his arms for over an hour, not saying a word, as we listened to the band that had closed the festival for the day. In many ways, I was so confused at how I was feeling. Grayson was a friend, nothing more, but he had always been able to calm me down and bring me back to neutral, but this time it was different. The way he'd held me just felt different.

I watched him walk around the front of his truck and open my door. Then I took his hand as I climbed out of the front seat. This time when I slid my hand in his, I felt a funny tingle through my body, especially when he placed his hand on my lower back to guide me up the front steps of my parents' house. When we got to the door, we both reached for the handle, but Grayson pulled his hand back and smiled at me.

"Sorry." He chuckled as I opened the door, and together we stepped into the living room.

"Ah, you guys are home. Dinner will be around eight," Mom called from the kitchen as we shut the front door.

"Hey, Mom. That sounds great. We are just going to go and get changed."

"Okay. I'm just getting ready to bake some cookies, if you two wanted to join me," she said, smiling.

"Sure. We'll be right up."

"How's Dad?'

"He's laying down upstairs. He will be okay. Don't you worry," Mom said, coming over to hug me. "Now, go get changed, and come on and help me bake."

Grayson and I walked down the stairs into the basement and entered our room. He walked over to where his bag was and began rooting through it, while I did the same. I looked over to where he stood. He was a handsome looking man, broad shoulders, strong chest, and for the very first time, I wondered to myself what it would be like to be underneath him, digging my fingers into his back. I swallowed hard and was about to thank him for today when he turned and looked my way.

"What's wrong?" he questioned, studying my face.

I swallowed hard and shook my head. "Nothing."

"You sure? You're looking at me funny."

I shrugged and pulled out a pair of pants and a T-shirt.

"Okay. Well, I'm just going to jump in the shower and get cleaned up before dinner."

Immediately, I felt my skin heat, and the scene flashed in my mind of him standing under the hot stream of water. "Okay, are you going to come and help in the kitchen?" I asked, my voice strained.

"Of course," he said, walking over to me and brushing a strand of loose hair behind my ear. "I'll be right up, as soon as I'm finished. Are you feeling okay? You're really flushed."

"Yeah, I'm fine." I swallowed hard.

He studied my eyes for a minute and then nodded. "Okay. See you up there," he said and turned, heading toward the bathroom.

As soon as he was gone, I looked at myself in the mirror and let out a deep breath. "You better stop thinking of him the way you are. It's only going to get your hurt," I whispered to myself and shook the thoughts of Grayson from my mind. I had no idea what this was that I was beginning to feel, but whatever it was it had to stop.

I quickly slipped out of my bathing suit and shorts and climbed into a pair of my favorite yoga pants and T-shirt and made my way upstairs.

Mom stood in the kitchen surrounded by ingredients and mixing bowls, studying a recipe in one of her books.

"What are you making?"

"You're favorite: double chocolate chip."

I smiled and sat down on the stool across from my mom. "Sounds great."

"So Grayson...he seems like he turned into a very nice young man."

"Dad hates him," I said.

"He doesn't. Your father is a stubborn man. You know that. Remember how long it took him to warm up to Rick."

"I guess." I shrugged.

"You guess what?" Grayson asked, coming up behind me, wrapping his arms around me, leaning down to kiss me on the cheek.

Instead of my body tensing this time at his touch, I allowed myself to relax in his arms and welcome him. "Nothing, so you're going to help us bake."

Grayson chuckled and sat down beside me. "I hate baking, but I will watch, maybe sneak a little raw batter like I normally do when you bake," he said, looking over at me and smiling.

"What? How do you hate to bake?" Mom asked, cracking two eggs into the bowl.

I couldn't help but giggle. "Mom, Grayson is more of a bagged mix kind of person. He believes all the ingredients should already be together and you just add a little water and mix," I said, looking over at Grayson and rolling my eyes.

"What is your problem? You've eaten the things I've made before," Grayson said in defense.

I giggled. "Yes, and I tell you every time to make them yourself. From scratch."

"Seriously, Grayson, you need to try it. It may seem like a mess at the beginning, but eventually all of the ingredients come together."

Jade walked into the kitchen at that exact moment and grinned. "What are we talking about?" she asked, coming over beside me and bumping me with her hip.

"Baking."

"Hmm, I see."

"I was just explaining to Grayson that everything seems like a mess at first, but eventually everything comes together," Mom said, dropping a cup of flour into the bowl in front of her.

"Yeah, you know, it's somewhat like a relationship. At first, it's a mess, but eventually you come together," she said, looking directly at me.

I felt my face heat as I met Grayson's eyes, and then I quickly averted my attention over to my mom. "Here, Mom, let me help," I said, pulling the recipe book in front of me.

Chapter 10

GRAYSON

We'd eaten dinner and were now all sitting around the table in the dining room listening to Rick and Jade talk about their upcoming wedding. Jean came into the dining room with the pot of coffee. "Anyone for more coffee?"

"I'm good thanks, Mom," Kendall answered, looking over at me then quickly averting her eyes.

"Grayson?"

"No, thank you, I'm good."

"Jade, Rick, it's your turn to clean up after dinner. Did either of you want any more before you start?"

"I might have some more in a little bit," Jade said, starting to collect plates.

"Okay, I will leave the pot on the warmer. What about you, Ryan?"

"None for me. I think I am going to go up and lay down," Ryan said, getting up from where he sat.

I looked over at him. He was still a little pale and a bead of sweat lined his forehead. "Are you feeling all right, sir?"

"I'm fine," he grumbled.

"Dad, maybe you should have Grayson check you over," Jade suggested as she stacked some serving bowls.

"As I said earlier, I don't need some young punk checking me over. Now, if you will excuse me, I am going to turn in."

"Daddy, Grayson is a doctor, and a good one," Kendall said, placing her hand on mine. "He does know what he is doing."

Ryan chuckled. "Yeah, doctor of what?" he said, turning to look over at me.

"Sir, I just graduated medical school at the top of my class. I'll be starting my internship in the cardiac unit..."

Ryan dismissed me and stood up from the table. "I thank you all for your concern, but I am fine. I just had a checkup, and I passed with flying colors. Now I am going to go upstairs and lay down. Good night, everyone."

Everyone was silent as Ryan climbed the stairs. I looked at Jean, who smiled softly at me, while she shook her head and mouthed "Don't worry about him." Jade and Rick both stood there looking over at the stairs, and then I looked over at Kendall. She hung her head, and when she looked up at me, I could see the hint of tears in her eyes. I knew she was worried, and I so badly wanted to wrap her in my arms and let her know everything would be okay.

"Well, on that note, I think I am going to take my coffee out to the back deck," Jean announced, taking her cup and heading out onto the patio. Jade and Rick picked up the dishes and took them into the kitchen, leaving Kendall and me alone.

She stood there, staring at the floor. I could tell she was fighting back tears. I walked over to her and placed one arm around her. "How would you like to go for a walk?"

She shook her head no. "I think I should go outside with my mom," she whispered as tears began to fill her eyes.

She stepped out of my embrace and was just about to the door when she stopped. I saw her wipe her eyes, and then her shoulders began to shake. I walked up behind her, placing my hands on her shoulders. "I think it's time we go and clear our heads," I whispered and took her hand in mine, leading her to the front door.

There were no complaints. She slipped her shoes on, and together we walked out the front door, pulling it closed behind us. We walked over to my truck, and I opened her door and helped her in, then I jogged around to the driver's side and hopped in, firing up the engine.

"Where are we going?"

"Just down to the lake," I said, reversing out of the driveway.

Once we arrived, I parked the car, and together we got out, but Kendall took off ahead of me and ran down to the water's edge. I jogged across the wet sand and was just about to let her know I was right behind her when she turned abruptly and collapsed in my arms, in full-blown tears.

I pulled her tightly against me and smoothed her hair as she cried into my chest. "I'm so worried about my dad," she sobbed. "I don't know why he is being so stubborn."

"Shhh. One thing I've learned in school is that you can't always help people. Sometimes they don't think they need it. You just need to hope that they get the help they need before it's too late."

She cried harder at my words. I knew that they were the truth and that was going to be hard for her to hear at this moment. She clung tightly to me until the tears finally slowed. "I know you're telling me the truth. It's just hard to accept right now." She sniffled.

"I know." I nodded and brushed a few strands of hair from her cheek. "How about we go for a bit of a walk before we head back?"

"Okay," she mumbled, and I slipped my hand in hers, and together we walked down the beach in the moonlight.

Chapter 11

KENDALL

We walked close to a mile before we turned around and headed back to where Grayson had parked his truck. We'd pulled into a coffee shop on our way back, and then we returned to the house. Everyone had already turned in for the night, and we both quietly made out way downstairs and got ready for bed.

I'd slipped into the bathroom to get ready for bed after Grayson. I washed my face, brushed my teeth, and got changed, then quietly opened the bedroom door, trying not to make any noise in case Grayson was already asleep. As I pushed the door open, I saw him lying on the floor in his makeshift bed with his hand behind his head, a book in the other hand.

"How was your shower?" he asked quietly.

"It was good. I expected you to be asleep."

"Just thought I'd do a little light reading before bed," he said, nodding to the book he held in his hands.

"Doesn't look like light reading to me," I said, nodding to the thick medical book he now had resting across his abs.

Grayson chuckled and placed the book down on the floor beside him and placed his other hand behind his head. I could feel his eyes on me as I crossed the room in my shorts and tank top and tucked my clothes into my bag. "I'm so used to reading this stuff. It's like you with one of your novels."

"I really don't see how you can compare the two." I giggled and pulled my book out of my bag, flashing him the cover of my romance novel before I crawled into the bed and curled up under the covers.

"I'll stick to my medical books, thanks." He chuckled, picking up the book again.

I had just begun reading when I heard Grayson groan, and I looked down to see he had rolled over onto his side, the book on the floor so he could read hands-free.

"You can't be very comfortable down there," I said in a low voice.

"It's fine. I'm good."

"No, really, if you want to you can sleep beside me."

Grayson sat up and looked over at me. "Kendall Roberts, are you trying to get me into bed with you?" he questioned, raising his eyebrows in gest.

I couldn't help but giggle. I wasn't sure what I was

doing by inviting him into this bed, but whatever it was it felt right. "No, not at all. I just feel bad that you are sleeping down on that hard floor."

"Seriously? That's the reason why you are offering? Are you trying to tell me that you don't want to sleep with this?" he questioned, gesturing with his hands toward his body.

I could feel my cheeks getting hot and knew that I had probably given away my thoughts from earlier, wondering what it would be like to be underneath him.

"Grayson, stop it. I don't mind sharing a bed with you," I said, swallowing hard.

"You're sure?"

"Of course. You have your side. I have mine." I looked into his eyes and pulled the blankets down on the opposite side of the bed and nodded toward the empty space. He didn't waste any time. He got up off the floor, grabbing his two pillows, and threw them down beside me, then closed his book and set it on the bedside table and crawled in.

He had barely even sat down and I could already feel an intense throbbing between my legs as excitement built. The scent of his cologne invaded my senses as he leaned back against his pillows and looked over at me. I had no idea what I was getting myself into.

"You're sure this is okay?" he asked.

I bit my bottom lip and nodded. The look on his face became series as his eyes washed over my face. I had to tear my eyes away from him, so I closed my book and placed it on my night table and reached up to shut the light off. When I lay back down I felt Grayson's arm under my head and my body stiffened.

"What are you doing?" I questioned.

"Going to sleep. What are you doing?" he mocked.

I rolled my eyes. "No, I mean what are you doing with your arm."

"Oh, I thought it might be nice to cuddle." He shrugged. "But we don't have to if you don't want to," he said, pulling his arm away.

"I didn't say that," I objected. "I guess it just took me by surprise."

"All right then, come here," he said, placing his arm across my pillow while waiting for me to snuggle into him.

I bit my bottom lip and cautiously snuggled into him, my heart beating hard as I wondered where the hell to put my arm. He didn't hesitate. Instead he grabbed my arm and rested it across his abs then he pulled me into him and held me tightly.

Every part of my body was on fire as I lay against him. I tried to calm myself down but could barely breathe, and every time I swallowed, I was sure he could hear it.

"You okay?" he asked, gently running his hand up my arm.

"Yes," I lied and tried to focus my attention on the sound of the steady beat of his heart.

"Nice isn't it," he whispered.

"Yes," I said, closing my eyes and slowly allowing my body to relax.

It wasn't long before Grayson was asleep, but I lay wide awake staring at the wall, wrapped in his arms. While a part of me wished this connection would never end, I couldn't help but wonder what it would be like after we got back to our normal lives. I knew he would go back to dating. He probably had a slew of girls lined up for when we returned, and I would go back to being the shoulder he cried on when things didn't work out between them. I closed my eyes and fought off the tears that were threatening to fall. I had no idea why such a large part of me wanted to be the girl he dated, and I knew I had to stop those feelings that I was having because in a matter of a few days we would be back in the city and I would be crushed.

Chapter 12

GRAYSON

"I can't believe we are going to see The Whiskey Barrels. I've been trying to get tickets to see them for the past two years! Who would have thought they would play at the Bear Creek Music Festival!" Jade said, jumping up and down in excitement in the middle of Steaming Cups as our favorite song by the band came on over the radio.

Both Rick and I tried to pretend that we weren't with the girls as they started dancing to the song that was playing on the radio. However, Jade and Kendall grabbed us and continued dancing, sending us both into a fit of laughter.

It was only a matter of a few more minutes when the barista signaled to us that our coffees were ready. Rick and I grabbed the cups, and then the four of us took a seat in one of the booths in the back. Once we were seated, Jade and Rick looked over at us, a sly smile on their faces.

"What?" I questioned.

"So, I want to know how the two of you lucked out and got stuck in the basement room?" Jade said, eying Kendall, who sat beside me stirring her coffee.

"What do you mean, Jade?" Kendall asked innocently, but I already knew where this conversation was headed.

"What I mean is that it's not fair that you guys can be as loud as you want and no one will hear. Rick practically has to put a pillow over my face every time we do it when we are home at Mom and Dad's."

"Jesus, Jade," Rick said, looking over at both of us and shaking his head. "Don't feel compelled to answer her," he said to both of us, "It will only egg her on more, and besides, no one needs to know the details of our sex life, and you don't need to know the details of theirs," Rick muttered, looking out the front window, a tinge of red on his cheeks at the questions Jade had put forth.

I couldn't help but chuckle. She wanted to play this game, two could play, I thought to myself. I reached for Kendall's hand and looked over at her then cleared my throat. She was probably going to kill me for this, but I was willing to take my chances, especially if it kept her nosiness at bay. "Don't be silly, it's fine. Jade, your sister and I are into some pretty kinky stuff," I said, looking over at Kendall whose eyes were wide as she waited for what was coming next. "You know, all that *Fifty Shades* type stuff? Well..." I chuckled, wrapping my arm around her. "She loves it when I'm rough with her, but I'm only rough if she is quiet."

Jade looked between us, her mouth hanging open in shock at my answer, and I picked up my coffee and took a sip. Rick, on the other hand, sat there grinning, but then I caught the look on Kendall's face and realized I'd probably taken this conversation about ten steps too far.

"Grayson, can you please move. I'd like to speak with you outside for a moment," she said, glaring at me.

I didn't argue. Instead, I got up from the table and held my hand out for her, but she refused to take it, climbing out of the booth and storming to the door. I looked over my shoulder at Rick and Jade and shrugged. "Looks like I might be in a little bit of trouble." I grinned and winked at Jade then followed Kendall outside.

I pulled the door open and walked over to where Kendall stood beside my truck, her back turned to me.

"Look, I'm sorry. I know my answer was far from appropriate, but she deserved that. She was way too far out of line.," I said, placing my hands on her upper arms.

"Far from appropriate? Is that what you're gonna call it? It was way over the line, Grayson."

"It might have been, but so was her question. It made you uncomfortable. I could see it, and I didn't like it."

"Yes, her question made me uncomfortable, but what you said, made me so much more than uncomfortable than her question ever could," she said, crossing her arms over her chest and pulling away from me.

"Look, I just gave her a little taste of her own medicine."

"A little taste? Jesus, that was a whole lotta taste, Grayson."

She turned her back on me and stood looking at the stores across the street. "I don't even know what you were thinking in there," she muttered.

"Okay, okay, I'm sorry. I won't do it again. It was totally inappropriate." Even though I'd apologized, Kendall still hadn't turned to look at me. I walked up behind her and wrapped my arm around her waist. "I mean it, I'm sorry," I whispered.

Kendall let out a breath and looked up at me, a look of displeasure on her face. "Fine, but please don't let it happen again."

Kendall stepped away and stormed back into the coffee shop, leaving me on the sidewalk. I knew she was pissed and was probably only forgiving me because we had to be around Jade and Rick all day. I blew out a breath and headed back inside, trying to figure out how to make things okay between us again.

WE SAT out on the back deck of her parents' house. Kendall and Jade sat at the edge of the pool, their feet dangling in the cool water, while Rick and I took a swim. I'd purchased The Whiskey Barrels' new album for

Kendall, and it was currently playing in the background. I'd actually sucked up to Kendall all afternoon, trying to smooth things over between us after this morning. Over the course of the afternoon, things had finally returned to normal with Kendall, and I and now she swam over to where she sat on the edge of the pool.

"You should come in," I said, placing my hands on her legs.

"Nah, I thought I might start a fire."

"YAY!" Jade yelled. "Let's play truth or dare!"

Kendall closed her eyes and blew out a deep breath and then looked up at me and shook her head. "Tell her no," she gritted. I could see she was afraid of what questions would pop up and what answers I might give.

"I'll be good, I promise." I grinned up at her and swam over to the ladder to get out of the pool.

"Who's up for truth or dare?" Jade shouted again.

"Bring it on, Jade," I called back and watched her run inside, returning with a bottle of tequila and a bowl of lemon slices.

"What is that for?" Kendall asked, wrapping herself in a towel before walking over and sitting down.

"Oh please tell me you've played this game before, my little not-so-innocent baby sister," Jade mocked.

I watched as Kendall rolled her eyes. "No, I haven't."

"Well, when it's your turn, you choose truth or dare, and one of us will ask you a question...If you want to skip your turn, then you drink a shot instead."

Kendall looked over to me. I knew she couldn't hold her alcohol very well, but I grabbed hold of her and pulled her into me, trying to assure her things would be fine.

"What do you say, are you going to play?" Jade asked, looking up at her sister.

"All right, fine. Let's do this."

Chapter 13

KENDALL

I'd passed on the first three rounds of the game, drinking back my shot each time. Grayson had passed on the first two questions and had only been asked who his celebrity crush was.

It was my turn again, and all eyes turned to me. I knew I couldn't handle another shot of tequila so soon, and I wasn't really sure about taking a dare.

"Truth or dare, Kendall?" Jade asked. "And you better choose something else other than a tequila shot or you're going to be down for the count." She giggled, knowing that I wasn't that much of a heavy drinker.

"Truth," I called out.

She squinted her eyes at me, and then a smile crept onto her face. "Okay, truth. What are your favorite positions?"

I felt my stomach turn and a sudden wave of heat

wash over my body as both Rick and Grayson looked over my way, waiting for my answer.

"Um...I choose dare," I said, trying to get out of answering.

"No way, you chose truth, so fess up."

"Um, doggie style," I said and glanced over to Grayson who seemed to be hanging onto my every word.

"All right, Jade, you're up," Grayson said, rubbing his hands together.

"I think I will pass this one," she said reaching for a freshly poured shot of tequila while Rick did the same.

"Okay, Grayson, your turn," Rick said. "Truth or dare?"

"Truth."

"How far back into Kendall's Instagram have you crept?"

Immediately, I lifted my head and looked over at Grayson. As soon as our eyes met, a light flush crept over his cheeks, and he suddenly seemed to be very uncomfortable. Grayson had always claimed that he didn't have time for any social media accounts because of his work load at school and now the hospital, but now, from the look on his face, that seemed to be untrue.

He cleared his throat and looked down at the pool deck between his feet. "I've, um, looked back pretty far," he answered without looking back at me.

"Really? How far?" Jade said, rubbing her hands together and looking over at me.

"I dunno, five years or so."

"Really, hmmm. All right, your turn there, little inno-cent one," Jade mocked. "Grayson, it's your question," she said, slapping him on the arm.

"Truth," I said, feeling a little bolder than I did the last time around, knowing that Grayson wouldn't ask me some-thing to embarrass me.

"What is your most favorite scar or birthmark, and where is it located?" he questioned.

Instantly, I felt a little calmer, since Grayson already knew the answer to this. I smiled. "It's the heart-shaped scar on the side of my leg, from that time I fell at the beach playing volleyball."

Grayson met my eyes and smiled. Again, both Rick and Jade passed, each taking another shot off the table. We now all sat there waiting for Grayson to answer the ques-tion Jade had been dying to ask since the last round.

"If I looked through your phone history, what would you be most embarrassed about?" she asked, looking over at me.

Grayson threw his head back and ran his hand over his face. It had been almost five minutes since Jade had asked the question when suddenly Grayson answered.

"I wouldn't be embarrassed about anything."

"Nothing at all?" Jade asked, shocked, her voice loud.

"No. Nothing. I have nothing to hide," Grayson answered, looking over at me.

"Let me see your phone then?" Jade said, standing up and holding her hand out. I watched as Grayson stood up and quickly typed his password into his phone and handed it over to Jade, who quickly started searching through his phone.

"Holy... How many girls have you been with?" she asked, searching through his messages.

"I've been with my fair share."

I was shocked at the twinge of jealousy that flew through me at his answer. Suddenly, the bathroom light in my parents' room caught my attention. "Shit, Mom and Dad are awake," I said, panicking and drinking down the last two shots of tequila that sat on the table.

"Whoa, Kendall, what are you doing?" Grayson said, taking his phone back from Jade and pocketing it quickly, then reaching over and taking the shot glasses from me.

"My goodness, you need to relax, sis. Now sit down. It's your turn," Jade said, rubbing her hands together, pouring four more shots and looking over at me. "Truth or dare?"

I looked at everyone, their eyes on me. I had no idea what she would ask if I said truth, so instead I took in a deep breath and looked over at her. "Dare."

"Ooooohh, getting ballsy are we. Dare..." she said, rubbing her hands together. "I want you to remove your bathing suit and go for a swim."

"For the love of God, Jade," Rick said, sitting forward. "Make the girl drink a couple of shots or something, kiss her boyfriend, but get naked in front of me??? Really???"

I looked over at my sister, a cruel smile on her lips. I

searched my brain, trying to figure out what it was she was getting back at me for, but I couldn't think of anything.

"Come on, Kendall."

I looked to Rick who looked down to the ground, then over to Grayson, who met my eyes. Then I looked over to Jade, who sat there looking pretty proud of herself. I knew why she was doing this.

"All right, I think the game is over," Grayson said, standing up and collecting the four full shot glasses, dumping the tequila on the grass.

"Oh come on. Our first dare of the night and you're going to pack it in."

"Yep, the night's done."

"I agree, Jade. I'm going to bed," Rick said, standing up and heading into the house. Jade started to pout and then went inside, following Rick up the stairs.

"I'll clean up," I said, taking the shot glasses from Grayson. "Go ahead. I'll be down in a minute."

"You sure?"

"Yep."

Grayson met my eyes, unsure of whether he should leave, and then made his way downstairs. I sat down on the chair and picked up the bottle of tequila, unscrewing the lid and pouring another two shots. I downed the first, then the second, and then poured a third. I couldn't believe my sister would do that, especially when she knew the truth, and then I downed the third shot.

GRAYSON

I was lying in bed reading when Kendall stumbled into the bedroom. She slurred something and then looked over at me. She looked a little pale.

"Are you okay?"

She nodded and then stumbled over to her bag, pulling out a pile of clothes. When she couldn't find what she was looking for, I could see frustration setting in. I got up out of bed and walked over to her. "What are you looking for?" I questioned.

"My pajamas," she said, giggling as she tripped over her slippers and almost fell. I grabbed her just in time and steadied her. She'd had a lot to drink tonight, and I knew she couldn't hold her alcohol well, but she hadn't appeared this drunk upstairs.

"Did you have more to drink after I came down here."

"Perhaps," she said, holding her fingers together signaling to me that she had a little more to drink.

"All right, let's get you into bed, shall we," I said, guiding her to sit on the edge of the bed, while I grabbed the shorts and T-shirt she slept in the night before and held them out to her.

She looked up to me and let out a loud hiccup, then started giggling as she slowly pulled her clothes from my hand. "Turn around," she said, looking up at me as she stood and pulled the button on her shorts open.

"Kendall, come on, just get changed," I said, afraid that she may fall over and hit her head while I had my back turned.

"Are you trying to see me naked?" she asked.

"No, I'm trying to make sure you don't crack your head open. Now come on."

"Not until you turn around."

"Fine," I said, holding my hands up and turning away from her.

"Thank you," she muttered, and I heard her shorts hit the floor, then her shirt floated down in front of me, a giggled hiccup escaping her again, and I seriously couldn't help myself. I wanted to turn around, but I held back. Then I heard her start to breathe a little harder and a groan escape her throat.

"You okay?" I questioned.

"I'm never playing this game with you again. This has got to be what alcohol poisoning feels like."

"You'd had enough before the game ended. No one told you to drink any more shots." I chuckled. "Really, I know you know your limits."

"Grayson, I don't feel so good," she said, her voice full of worry.

I turned around quickly. Kendall stood there facing me, her bra in her hand as she tried to cover herself with her arms.

She looked at me as she continued trying to cover her body. "I told you not to turn—" Her hands immediately went from trying to cover her body to her mouth and she began to heave. I wasted no time. I wrapped my arm around her waist and rushed her out the door into the bathroom, pulling her hair back just in time for her to empty the contents of her stomach into the toilet.

"Oh my God," she said in between heaves. "I'm so embarrassed."

"Shhhh, it's okay," I soothed.

"God, go away. I want to die," she said as she heaved once again, emptying the contents of her stomach into the toilet.

"I'm going to go upstairs and grab you something for your stomach. Just stay here and put this cool cloth on your head, okay."

I snuck up the stairs and rounded the corner into the kitchen to see Jean standing there with a cup of tea in her hand.

"Grayson, what are you doing up?" she asked quietly.

"Kendall, she's a little under the weather."

"Oh, yes, I saw the almost empty bottle. Is she all right?"

"Yeah I just need a glass of water and a couple headache tablets."

"You can find those in the cupboard above the fridge."

I nodded and went about getting the water and tablets, and then I made my way back downstairs. Kendall was already in bed curled up on her side.

"Here, have these and a few sips of water," I said, sitting down on my side of the bed. As soon as she'd taken the tablets, I relaxed back against the pillows and waited until I was sure she was okay. She drifted off to sleep in a matter of minutes.

WE PASSED on the concert the next morning, and together we lay in bed watching *Bridesmaids*, one of Kendall's favorite movies. She was curled up into my side and rested her head on my chest, my arm instantly going around her.

"You are way too good to me," she murmured as I pulled the covers up over her cold shoulder and pulled her tight against me. She'd been cold all morning, and the last thing I'd wanted was for her to get sick.

"What?"

"You are too good for me. Coming with me this weekend with no complaints, putting up with my family, especially Jade, right down to holding my hair back last night."

"You should know me by now, Kendall. I don't do things I don't want to."

Kendall started to laugh. "As if you didn't have any other better offers this weekend, and now look, I feel like this is your punishment. You came to see a music festival, and here you are stuck in bed with me watching rom-coms because I'm completely hungover."

"First, I'm pretty sure my punishment was last night, while having to hold your hair back and watch you puke your brains out?" I chuckled.

Kendall shrugged, then rested her chin on her fist and looked up at me. "Ugh, don't remind me, but I wasn't talking about that. I meant watching rom-coms."

"Mmmm, I see," I said, pushing the few strands of loose hair out of her eyes. "Well, what if I told you that I actually like rom-coms?" I said, studying her eyes.

She looked back at me with an unsure look in her eyes. "Then perhaps we will need to find you a new punishment."

"What if I also told you that I really didn't have any better offers this weekend, and even if I did, I still would have come here and spent the weekend with you?" I said in a low voice, cupping her cheek and meeting her eyes.

"What are you saying?" she murmured, unsure of where I was going with this.

I studied her eyes, and without saying anything, I placed my fingers under her chin, tilted her head back, and slowly brought my lips to hers.

Chapter 15

KENDALL

I sat between Grayson's legs, leaning back against his chest, and listened while Inflated Young played their last set of songs for the night. We'd finally decided to come down to the park once the sun had gone down to spend the evening with Jade and Rick. Jade had gone to grab some food, while Rick and Grayson were deep in a conversation.

I listened to the lyrics of my favorite song, and I was immediately brought back to this morning when Grayson had so gently kissed me. I hadn't been able to get that kiss off my mind today. The way his hand gently cupped my cheek, followed by his lips dancing over mine, his tongue washing through my mouth. The rumors that had floated around the cafeteria at the hospital were true—Grayson was an amazing kisser.

Closing my eyes, I just got lost in that feeling once

again. When I felt a familiar throb between my legs, I opened my eyes and let out a breath, sitting up. Immediately, I felt Grayson's hand on my arm. "You feeling okay?" he asked, concern lining his voice.

When I had mentioned coming down here, he had originally said no because he was so worried about me bring so dehydrated from last night. He didn't want me out in the heat, but I insisted. So he compromised. We could go if I promised to make sure to fill up on water and electrolyte drinks.

"Yeah, just going to use the ladies' room and get some more water. Did you want anything?"

"I'm good. Did you want me to come with you?" he questioned.

"I'll be fine. Stay with Rick." I smiled.

"Okay. Just be careful."

"I will be. I'll be right back."

It had taken me almost twenty minutes to find a washroom that wasn't overcrowded and then a drink vendor. I grabbed a water and was about to make my way back when I began to feel dizzy, so I decided to sit down on the edge of the park under one of the empty gazebos. Once seated, I looked up at all the white twinkling lights they had been decorated with. I'd always thought these were so romantic decorated like this. I smiled to myself as Grayson started to invade my thoughts.

As the music played, I thought back to this morning once

again and the way he'd looked at me right before he'd kissed me. He'd never looked at me before the way I'd at one point looked at him. It wasn't a secret the guy was attractive, and like any girl with a set of raging hormones, I, too, had thought it, but when I realized he only looked at me as a friend, I quickly pushed down how I felt about him and never thought of him that way again. Until now. I was confused by his confession, that even if he'd had something better this weekend, this was where he wanted to be. I swallowed hard. I couldn't allow myself to think there was something more than there was between us. That was how I got crushed.

I was pulled from my thoughts abruptly when the music stopped and they announced The Whiskey Barrels would be coming up in a few short minutes. I glanced down at my watch and realized I'd been gone close to almost forty minutes, and I knew that Grayson would probably be wondering where I was.

I drank down the last couple mouthfuls of water and had just stood up when I saw Grayson walking my way.

"There you are," he said, coming over to me and taking my hands in his.

"Sorry. I really needed that water."

"You feeling okay?" he asked, looking down into my eyes with concern.

"Yeah, I was just feeling a little dizzy, but I'm good now," I said, smiling up at him, only he didn't smile back. Instead, his eyes were lined with concern.

"Come, let's just sit down here," he said, pulling me back toward the gazebo.

"What about Jade and Rick?"

"They are holding our spot."

"But The Whiskey Barrels will be playing soon."

"We got time. I just want to talk to you for a minute," he said, patting the spot beside him.

We both sat there in silence for a few moments, and then "Flying Without Wings" by Westlife started playing. Grayson looked at me, stood up, and held his hand out for me to take. "Dance with me."

"What?" I asked, shock lining my voice.

"Dance with me," he said, grabbing my hands.

"Grayson, I don't dance." I giggled, but he pulled me up into a standing position anyways.

"Come on."

He helped me up the steps and waited while I stepped up into the gazebo, then he pulled me into his arms and held me tightly against him. The instant our bodies touched, I felt a wave of excitement go through my body.

I felt like I was fifteen again at my first high school dance. I was nervous and had no idea where to put my hands, yet Grayson slid his hands into place around my waist as if they belonged on me. Then I heard him start to chuckle.

"What?"

"Would you relax a little," he said with a smile. "God, it's like you've never danced with me before."

I nervously giggled, and then finally I slowly rested both arms on his shoulders, took in a deep breath, and allowed myself to finally relax and my body to sway to the soft music.

"I want you to know that I meant what I said this morning."

I looked up into his eyes, unsure of what it was he was speaking of. "Oh?"

"About coming with you this weekend."

I wasn't sure how to respond to him, and a deep silence grew between us as he looked deep into my eyes. Ever so slowly, he began moving into me, and I was sure was just about to kiss me, when I heard Jade calling my name. I pulled out of his arms and turned to see my sister.

"Hey, Jade, over here!" I yelled out.

"The band's about to start, come on."

I turned and looked back at Grayson. His face took on an annoyed look as he looked at me, and then he smiled and waved at Jade. "We were just about to head back," he said, stepping up beside me.

GRAYSON

Once the festival ended, the four of us returned to the house and relaxed in the hot tub on the back deck. Soft music played in the background, and I rested my head back on the edge of the hot tub and allowed the heat to sink into my body when I felt Kendall slip her hand into mine. I looked over at her, and she gave me a soft smile.

"Well, we are headed to bed, guys," Jade whispered, climbing out of the hot tub.

"Want some help putting the cover back on?" Rick asked.

"That would be great."

I helped Kendall out of the tub and watched as she grabbed her towel, wrapping it around her bikini-clad body, her and Jade grabbing any dishes we'd had out on the back deck, and heading inside. Rick and I lifted the lid onto the tub, and then we, too, ventured inside.

I quietly walked down the basement steps and opened the bedroom door. Kendall stood with her back to me, and I watched as she reached behind her neck and pulled at one of her bikini strings, untying it. She had no idea I was standing there, and at first it felt wrong, but then I felt my cock jump at the thought of possibly seeing her naked. She pulled at one of the other strings, but instead of it falling away from her body, the strings knotted.

"Shit," she muttered under her breath, dropping the towel she'd been holding against her so she could use both hands to try and untie the knot.

"Need some help?" I asked quietly, shutting the door behind me.

She turned, a rush of pink hitting her cheeks as she reached for the towel that lay on the bed.

"Oh, I'm sorry. I didn't think you'd be down here this soon," she said, swallowing hard, trying to hide her embarrassment.

"Don't be sorry. Do you need help?" I repeated quietly.

She hesitated a minute before answering, "Would you mind?"

I didn't say anything. Instead, I stepped forward and started to work at the tangled strings, finally getting them to a point that I was able to undo the knot. As the material fell away from her body, Kendall grabbed the towel that lay on the bed and pulled it up to her chest.

I should have stepped away and allowed her to leave and head to the washroom to finish changing, but instead my hands lingered on her wet skin. My heart pounded and my breathing quickened as my hands trailed down her back and I slid my hands on her hips. My cock was hard, and a jolt of electricity went through me as my fingers lingered on the soft skin of her hips. I could feel her tensing, and I was afraid she was going to dart out of my reach, but she didn't move.

I stepped closer, gripping her sides, the sweet smell of her skin invading my senses. I wanted her, and my cock throbbed at the thought of actually having her. I slowly leaned in and placed a kiss on the side of her neck as my hands gripped her hips. My lips danced over her neck, and I heard a soft gasp come from her lips as she tilted her head to the side to give me more access. I continued kissing her neck, while I inched my right hand to rest on her lower abdomen.

"What...what are we doing?" she asked, breathless.

I pulled my lips from her neck, but I didn't answer her. Instead, I took my left hand and gently turned her head so she was able to look at me, and bent down and met her lips, kissing her deeply.

The towel she'd been holding dropped in a pile on the floor at our feet and she spun in my arms, turning her body into me. She wrapped her arms around my neck and continued kissing me. I pulled her tightly against me, my tongue parting her lips and washing through her mouth. A soft moan escaped her. My cock, now hard as a rock, throbbed when the sound of her moan hit my ears, and I pulled her even tighter against me so she could feel me.

Our lips parted and I looked down into her eyes, as my fingers found the sides of her bikini bottom. She looked down and watched as I gently pulled at the strings. I expected her to tell me no, but she didn't flinch as the material fell away from her body and to our feet. I couldn't help but allow my eyes to roam as much of her body as I could see. She stood there, her cheeks flushed, biting her bottom lip as she reached down between us and pulled at the drawstring of my suit and pushed it off my hips. As I sprung free, I watched that rosy flush creep across her upper chest.

"You okay? I whispered, swallowing hard. I wanted to make sure she wanted this just as much as I did because once we crossed this line, there would be no going back.

She bit her bottom lip and nodded and looked up at me with innocent eyes. I leaned in and met her lips, and she surprised me by taking my hand in hers and placing it on her breast.

I backed us up to the edge of the bed and pulled her down with me, covering us both. She lay partially under me, as I propped myself up on my forearm to be able to look down on her. I looked down into her eyes as my free hand explored her body.

I inhaled deeply when I felt her hand take my cock and stroke it slowly as she looked up into my eyes. I leaned down and kissed her lips to keep myself from moaning. I wanted to be inside of her so badly, hearing that sweet moan I'd heard earlier as I slowly pumped into her. I slid my hand down and ran my fingers through her slick heat. She closed her eyes, bit her bottom lip, and tilted her head back as I ran my fingers over her swollen bud. She parted her legs a little farther, allowing me to slide a finger inside of her. She was so tight, and I so badly wanted to feel her wrapped around me. When I slipped a second finger inside of her, her hand left my cock and she gripped my bicep.

"I want to feel you," I whispered, kissing her again, then pulling away, looking down into her heady eyes.

"I do too," she whispered.

"I don't have—"

She placed a single finger on my lips, shushing me. "I'm on the pill," she whispered.

"You're sure?"

She looked up into my eyes, saying nothing, and nodded. I reached down between us, stroked my cock a couple of times. As I ran my cock through her juices, she let out a soft moan, and as I placed myself at her opening and began pushing, she gripped my back.

She was tighter than I imagined, and she let out a moan that sounded like pleasure mixed with pain. I slowed down a little, pulling back. "Are you okay?" I questioned.

She blushed a little at my question, and then looked at me. "Just take your time. You're..."

"I'm what?" I asked.

"Nothing, just go slow," she whispered.

I placed myself at her opening again and kissed her deeply. I slowly entered her and began to pump gently into her. She moaned beneath me as I held her tightly against me. A loud moan escaped her lips as I pumped deeply into her.

"Kendall, you've got to be quiet," I whispered in a breathless voice. "You'll wake the whole house."

She let out another moan as she tightened around me and placed her hand up by her mouth. I knew she was close, and I could already feel my own release building.

I met her lips to try to quiet her down, but it did little good as her body tensed beneath me. As I felt the gush of heat, I pumped a few more times and felt my body tense as my release hit. I poured myself into her and collapsed on her, breathing hard.

KENDALL

I rolled over and felt the familiar ache between my legs, reminding me of what happened between Grayson and I last night. I opened my eyes and stared at the light-green walls of the downstairs bedroom, then rolled over and was surprised to find the bed was empty, Grayson already gone. I sat up and looked around the room. The pile of clothes Grayson had placed on the back of the chair in the corner was gone, along with his bag. I glanced over to the door and saw his bag sitting there, already packed and ready to go by the door.

I sat up, pulling the covers around me. I had expected to wake up this morning to a sleeping Grayson. Instead, I woke to an empty bed. I could feel anxiety creeping into my chest as panic began to set in.

I threw the cover back and climbed out of the bed and went to pull the covers back over the bed when I saw a few drops of blood on the sheets. I threw on a T-shirt and quickly stripped the bed and took everything and placed it into the washer. Then I went back to the bedroom and grabbed a change of clothes and the towel on the floor and headed to the washroom. As soon as the hot water hit my skin in the shower, the tears began to flow. I leaned against the wall and cried into my hands. The thought of him regretting last night almost made me sick to my stomach. What if he had seen the blood? Surely, he would know what that meant, and embarrassment flooded through me. I sat down on the floor of the shower and cried, letting out all the feelings I was holding onto.

I'd just stepped out of the shower when I heard Jade outside the bathroom door. "Bout time you're up. We're gonna head to Steaming Cups. You coming?"

I looked at my reflection, taking in my red, swollen eyes. I swallowed hard and took a deep breath and did my best to sound better than I felt. "Can you give me twenty minutes?"

"Yep, no problem."

I dried off and got dressed and then did my best to cover up the mess that I was with makeup that I hardly ever wore. Once I was satisfied, I went back to the bedroom and shoved all my stuff messily into my bag, placing it besides Grayson's on the floor.

The four of us walked to Steaming Cups. Jade and Rick walked in front, keeping the conversation alive, while Grayson and I walked behind them. He'd barely glanced my way this morning as he mumbled good morning to me when I'd walked upstairs. Now he walked with his hands shoved deeply into his pockets, his head down, barely contributing anything to the conversation.

"We are getting you two breakfast. Why don't you guys get a seat."

"No, it's okay. I'll get our breakfast," Grayson said, glancing over at me, then quickly averting his eyes.

"No, man, really. You guys got our drinks last night. This is on us," Rick said.

Grayson turned to me and placed his hand on my lower back, guiding me over to an empty booth, and waited for me to take a seat. We sat there in silence beside one another until Jade and Rick arrived, one carrying a try full of hot coffees, the other a tray full of breakfast sandwiches.

Jade and Rick had done all the talking through breakfast, while both Grayson and I sat and listened, nodding our heads occasionally to what it was that they were saying. I could feel the tension pouring off him as he still hadn't looked my way. Did he regret last night?

I'd just taken the last bite of my sandwich when Jade set her coffee mug down on the table. "All right, I don't know what is going on between the two of you, but something is different," she spit out.

I glanced over to Grayson, who looked to me, then he turned to Jade. "It was just a long day yesterday, being out in the heat," he answered.

Jade looked to me to certify his answer, which I nodded my head. "Yeah I'm still not feeling all that great," I lied. Which really wasn't a lie, it was the truth, but it wasn't the reason that she thought.

"I see. Well, I guess we should get home, let you two get on the road."

"Yeah, I'm sure traffic will be a bitch," Rick said in agreement.

"Yeah, you're probably right, especially with most people leaving Bear Creek today," Grayson said. "The last thing I want is to be stuck in a truck for hours on end."

My eyes burned at Grayson's statement. He didn't want to be trapped in a truck with me for hours. I totally knew now that I was right. He regretted last night and probably couldn't wait to get me out of his face. I fought tears the entire walk back and had never been so happy to see my parents' driveway.

We'd loaded our things into the back of Grayson's truck and went inside to say our good-byes then we piled into his truck and Grayson reversed out of the driveway and sped off toward the highway.

Just as we turned onto the highway, I glanced over at Grayson. His eyes were trained on the road, and I was about to say something when he leaned forward and turned up the music on the radio. Instead of saying anything, I sat back in the seat and readied myself for a long, quiet drive home.

Traffic had been horrendous, the tension in the cab

was unbearable, and I had never been so happy to see my apartment building coming up into view in my life. Throughout the course of the day, my mood deteriorated. I had gotten my hopes up that Grayson would want to be with me as much as I wanted to be with him, but since he had been silent towards me most of the day, I was quickly seeing that that wasn't the case. I was going to tell him just to let me out in front of the building, but before I could, he pulled into the parking lot, pulled the truck into a spot, and cut the engine.

"I'll help you take your stuff up," he said, climbing out of the truck. Unlike at my parents', he didn't come around and open my door to help me out. Instead, he went directly to the back and pulled out my bag and stood there waiting for me. I let out a breath, unhitched my seatbelt, and climbed out of the truck.

"Really, you don't need to," I said, trying to take the bag from him. "I know you're tired."

"It's fine," he barked. Instead of handing over the bag, he pulled it away from me and placed his hand on the small of my back, ushering me forward.

The tension between us in the elevator was beyond excruciating. He stood across from me, his body stiff as he avoided eye contact with me. I had never been so happy to hear the *ding* of the elevator signaling we'd arrived on my floor. I walked down the hall, slipped my key into the lock, and pushed the door open. I really just wanted him to drop my bag and go—it would be easier—but instead,

Grayson walked inside and placed my bag down on the floor. I stood there, not sure what I should do or what to even say, when he turned his eyes on me.

"Well, I guess this is it. Thank you for the weekend," he said, taking a step forward and pulling me in for a hug.

I hugged him back gently. "You are welcome," I murmured. "What is your week like?" I had no idea why I asked that. Maybe it was to try and certify how it was I was feeling.

"Busy. I start at the hospital tomorrow. Apparently, it's twelve-hour days, but I've been forewarned that the doctor I'm under puts in about fourteen hours. What about you?"

"I have training on the new booking system this week."

"Ah, so I probably won't see you in the cafeteria."

"Probably not." We both stood there in silence, looking at one another. "Well, when you get time, call me."

"No promises on when, but I will," he said, leaning down and placing a single kiss on my lips. I swallowed hard, doing my best to choke back the tears that were about to fall from my eyes any second.

He turned and made his way to the door and didn't look back. I wanted to scream at him to stop and not to leave. I wanted to tell him that I was crushed, that he'd hurt me, but instead, I said nothing, and when I heard the door click behind him and silence fill my apartment, I buried my face in my hands and let the tears fall.

Chapter 18

GRAYSON

I dropped my bag onto my bed and quickly emptied the contents, then I made my way to the kitchen and opened the fridge. I stared at the contents, finding nothing that even remotely sparked my appetite. I wandered back to the bedroom and flopped down on the bed, rubbing the back of my neck with my hand. I was exhausted from the drive and from the stress I'd been carrying all day.

It had started early this morning. I'd woken up, Kendall was sound asleep beside me. I watched her for a while, taking in her beauty. She was absolutely beautiful, and that was when the moment of truth had hit. I was in love with my best friend. It was then I realized that was why no relationship ever worked out for me, because no matter what the girls were like, I had spent every moment comparing them to Kendall.

While I tried to allow those thoughts to settle in my

mind, she rolled over onto her side. Then more panic set in. How would I tell her? What if she didn't return my feelings? I was finding it hard to breathe and kicked the covers back and got up out of bed. I figured I'd go take a hot shower and try to relax, but when I turned back to the bed, that was when I had seen a few spots of blood on the sheets. The tightness in my chest took over. I'd known Kendall my entire life. I'd known her dating history, and the way she spoke, I never in my wildest dreams would have believed she was a virgin.

Instead of proceeding with my shower, I quickly dressed and packed up my bag. As I slipped out the bedroom door, I threw my shirt on over my head. I was just about to walk up the stairs when I stopped. What kind of man was I being? Kendall would wake and find me gone.

I turned and faced the door, opening it up a little bit to see her still asleep. She was absolutely breathtaking. I stepped inside the door and walked over to her side of the bed. I wanted to wake her with a kiss and stop being a coward, but as the seconds passed, the air became so thick I could barely breathe. I had no idea what I had done. Instead of kissing her, I panicked and left the room, making my way upstairs.

As the morning went on, I grew even more silent, and once she had joined the rest of the family, I could barely even look at her. I would have done things so much differently had I known the truth. I would have taken my time with her. Perhaps it wouldn't have happened at all, until I knew she was for sure ready. I'd spent the entire day in silence with the girl I loved, and I could have kicked myself for it.

I had hoped she would have mistaken my quietness for a bad mood, and I had given her every chance to invite me to stay the night at her place. I insisted on taking her bags up to her apartment. I had come in and tried the idle chitchat, which I apparently sucked at, but instead, she let me leave without as much as a word to me. Instead of taking control, I'd left her apartment and driven home convinced that I'd blown my chance with her and, knowing Kendall, left her thinking I had gotten what I wanted.

I lay back on my bed and closed my eyes, thinking back to last night. Thinking back to her plea for me to go slow. Then the look on her face and the way she clung to me as she came. I ran my hand over my face and got up off the bed. I needed to either stop thinking of it or call her.

I went in search of my cell phone, finally finding it on the kitchen table where I'd dropped it beside my wallet and keys and picked it up. I opened up my messages and quickly typed out a silly message as to why I wanted to see her, instead of just telling her the truth, and was about to send it when something stopped me. There was no way I should do this through a text. Instead, I grabbed my keys, pocketed my wallet, and made my way out the front door.

I drove across town to her building and parked my

truck in the visitors' section. Then I made my way across the parking lot to the front door, first looking up at her fifth-story windows. The apartment was completely dark, and then I glanced to where she normally parked. Her car was gone. I turned around and made my way back to my truck. I wasn't going home. I was going to sit here and wait until she returned from wherever it was she had gone.

I finally gave up at three in the morning. There had been no sight of her. I had even sent her a message a little after one, with no response. I had blown it, and I had no one to blame but myself.

KENDALL

The week had dragged on, and by Friday, I was exhausted. I hadn't heard from Grayson all week, except for a very strange text message he had left me the night we had gotten home from Bear Creek. I hadn't bothered to return the message, since I was still hurt and really had nothing to say to him.

I was so glad it was finally Friday. It had been a long day to wrap up all the training, and I trudged down the hall to my apartment carrying two full bags of groceries. I placed the bags down on the counter and had started to put things away when my cell phone rang.

I glanced over to the screen and was surprised to see Jade's number. She didn't normally call during her work hours. I reached for the phone and answered.

"Hello."

"Kendall, thank God. I've been trying to call you," Jade said, breathless.

Instantly, my body sprang into high alert. Jade sounded on the verge of tears. "Sorry, I left my phone at home today. What's wrong?"

"It's Dad," she choked out, and then I heard a sob escape her mouth. Panic instantly filled my body, and then I heard Rick's voice.

"Hey, Kendall," Rick said, taking the phone from Jade. "Your dad has been admitted into the hospital with severe chest pains. I'm going to come and pick you up. Jade will stay here with your mom. Can you be ready in ten?"

My chest started to hurt as the adrenaline ran through my veins. "Um, okay, yeah, I will meet you downstairs," I bit out, hanging up the phone.

I looked around the apartment, forgetting what I'd been doing, and reached for my purse. I grabbed my keys from the table and my sweatshirt that hung on the hook just inside the door and rushed downstairs.

Rick was there within minutes, and I hopped into the car, and we sped off toward the hospital. We rushed to the emergency room and found Mom and Jade sitting together holding hands.

"What happened?" I asked, frantic.

"He was outside in the garden and he...he just collapsed," Mom answered. "He went down like a tonne of bricks, gripping his chest."

"My God," I gasped. "How is he? Have you heard anything?" I asked, panicked.

"We know nothing. No one has come to talk to us yet," Mom said, tears filling her eyes.

"They were running tests when I called you," Jade answered.

I nodded. "Who's the doctor?"

Both Jade and Rick looked at me and shrugged. "It was a nurse who came out to tell us."

I was about to go to the nurses' station to see what I could find out when Grayson rounded the corner followed by Dr. Simpson. I could barely breathe as Grayson locked eyes with me and turned to say something to Dr. Simpson. I watched as both men turned and looked over at me, then he said something to Grayson before he turned the other way and left. Dr. Simpson, however, continued down the hall towards us.

"Mrs. Roberts," Dr. Simpson said, approaching us, holding his hand out, "your husband is finally stable."

"Oh, thank God."

"With that said, we are getting ready to perform emergency bypass surgery. The operation will take about three to six hours. I will get one of the nurses to direct you to the more comfortable waiting lounge, and we will notify you as soon as the operation is finished and Mr. Roberts is in recovery."

Mom turned to us and asked for a minute alone with the doctor, sending us off to the side.

I sat down next to Jade and leaned back against the wall.

"So why didn't Grayson come over?" Jade questioned almost immediately.

I let out a breath. "Probably because he can't be apart of this, being that he knows the person, not to mention the family," I said.

"Yeah, but I mean, he could have come just to make sure that you are okay."

I knew exactly why Grayson didn't come over to see us. I knew it all too well. He had gotten what he wanted, and I had to live with the fact that my best friend had made me believe there was a glimmer of something more between us than their actually were. I shrugged it off. "It's okay. I will meet up with him in a few," I lied.

Two hours later, we were all seated in the quiet lounge. I lay on the couch watching an episode of *Three's Company*. Jade and Rick had just returned from the cafeteria with a hot cup of tea and a sandwich for Mom.

"You sure you didn't want anything?" Mom asked, looking over at me.

I looked to the sandwich and my stomach growled. "Maybe I will go and get something," I said, getting up off the couch.

"Did you want company?" Jade asked.

"No, I'll be all right. You guys stay with Mom," I said, leaving the room.

I wandered the quiet halls down to the cafeteria and

walked into the little shop that was run by the volunteers of the hospital. I grabbed a green tea, a grapefruit cup, and an egg salad sandwich, and then went and grabbed a table off in the corner.

I had just taken a bite into my sandwich when I heard someone clear their throat behind me. "Want some company?"

I turned to see Grayson standing there, a hot cup of coffee in his hand.

I shrugged, not really sure if I wanted his company or not, but he placed his coffee down on the table anyways, and then pulled the chair around to sit right beside me. Once seated, he looked at me, then hung his head. "Are you okay?"

I nodded. "Dad's in surgery. Apparently, he collapsed in the garden."

"I know."

"I saw you earlier. Why didn't you come over?"

"I couldn't. I explained to Dr. Simpson the situation and he advised against it. So I went and joined the other specialist. I was going to message you, but this is the first time I've gotten a break all night."

I grew quiet as Grayson took my hands in his. We sat there like that for a few moments. "Is he going to be okay?"

Grayson looked to me. "If it's any consolation, Dr. Simpson is one of the best heart surgeons in this entire hospital. He's in good hands, Kendall."

"I know." I nodded, still not sure why Grayson hadn't let go of my hands.

"Are we okay?"

I looked up at him. A look was reflected in his eyes I had never seen before. "What do you mean?"

"Exactly that...are we okay?"

I shrugged, looking down at the sandwich I had no desire to eat. "I don't know." That was all I could say. I had no idea how he felt.

Grayson blew out a breath as the pager attached to his shirt went off. "You really should eat. I have to get back to work. I'm supposed to be done at two. You should have heard by then how your Dad is. I can come around and take you home."

I shook my head. "It's okay. You don't need to do that. I know you'll be tired. Rick and Jade can take me," I answered.

Grayson met my eyes and shook his head. "I want to."

Grayson stood up and went to walk away, but instead turned back, leaned down, and placed a long, lingering kiss on my cheek, then picked up his coffee and made his way over to the elevator.

I sat there for a while, and then picked up my sandwich and took a bite. Grayson hadn't been gone long when I felt a small hand on my shoulder. I turned to see Jade standing there.

"Hey."

"We were getting worried. You'd been gone for so long, but then I saw why."

I nodded, wiping a tear off my cheek.

"What's going on with the two of you?"

"What do you mean?" I asked, trying to play it off as nothing.

Jade looked at me, squinting her eyes a little. It was like she would be able to see me clearer and know that I was lying to her. "I know you told me that there wasn't anything between the two of you, but I don't believe that anymore."

"Oh yeah, why is that?" I questioned.

"Because something happened between the two of you the other night up at the cottage."

I looked at Jade, trying my best not to get flustered, and shook my head. "No."

"Kendall, I forgot to give you back your iPOD at the festival. I decided to bring it downstairs the other night. I, um, I heard."

"OH, MY GOD," I said, burying my face in my hands to hide my embarrassment.

"Don't be embarrassed. The pair of you were all over one another when you claimed you weren't dating, and it was like complete energy reversal afterward. Why are the two of you not together?"

"I don't know. He barely spoke to me the next day. I

felt confused enough. He drove me home, and then we just went our separate ways."

Jade nodded in understanding and softly smiled. "Sounds to me that you both are having a case of the morning-after jitters?"

I frowned and looked over at Jade, unsure of what she was talking about. "What?"

"I call it the morning-after jitters. Neither of you have ever felt this way about someone before, and you have no idea how to react. So you push one another away. Rick and I were the same way when we first got together."

"I see. How did you guys get over it?" I questioned.

"Well, I heard him ask you if you needed a ride home tonight."

"He did."

"What was it you said?"

"You were apparently listening. You tell me?" I asked, pissed that my sister had been eavesdropping on apparently more than this conversation.

"You said we would take you, but I hate to inform you we won't. So I guess you will need a ride home from him. So you better send him a text and let him know," Jade said, standing up. "Now we better get upstairs."

"Jade!" I demanded.

"You asked me how Rick and I got over it. I am just pushing you in the direction to help you both."

I frowned. I was angry at my sister, but I knew her heart was in the right place. I stood up, taking my garbage and throwing it in the trash on our way to the elevator. Once there, I pulled out my phone and quickly sent a text to Grayson.

The four of us had been waiting in the lounge for what felt like hours when we finally saw Dr. Simpson walk in. He went over and sat down with Mom while Rick stood off to the side listening. Mom got up to follow Dr. Simpson to go and see Dad, and Rick came over to us.

"Well?"

"Your dad is out of recovery. Surgery went well. Looks like he is going to be fine."

Immediately, a sense of relief washed over me. The words Rick had spoken were like music to my ears, and I turned to Jade and gave her a hug. We waited patiently for Mom to return, and when she did, we each went over and wrapped our arms around her.

"I think that you girls should get home and get some rest," Mom said, brushing a loose strand of hair from my eyes.

"You, too, Mom. You'll come and stay with Rick and I," Jade said immediately.

"What about you, Kendall?"

I looked over at Jade and then to Rick and was about to ask for a ride when I heard a familiar voice behind me.

"I'll take her home," Grayson said, stepping into the lounge.

Chapter 20

GRAYSON

I'd taken a few moments to talk with Kendall's family, and then we made our way through the hospital and to my car. We drove through the quiet city over to her apartment, and I climbed out of the truck, walking over to her side and opening the door. We rode the elevator in silence, and I followed behind her down the hall and waited as she slid her key in the lock. When I had gotten her text that she needed a ride, I had made up my mind that the night wasn't going to pass us by without me letting her know how I felt about her.

I followed her into her apartment and closed the door behind me, locking the deadbolt. "Oh God, my groceries," she said as she stood just inside the kitchen looking at the mess of what appeared to be melted ice cream on the floor. "Jade called, and I rushed out of here. I forgot to put all the fridge and freezer stuff away," she cried, going in to start cleaning up, but instead I stopped her.

"It's okay. I got it. Why don't you go and take a hot shower. I will clean up this mess," I said, digging into the bags to see what could be salvaged after sitting out in the warmth for the seven hours she'd been at the hospital.

I was about to turn to grab the garbage pail and some cleaner and paper towels and saw her standing there watching me. "Kendall, I got it. Go."

She looked at me a little longer, then nodded and made her way down the hall. I spent the next twenty minutes cleaning up the mess of spoiled meat, melted ice cream and ruined yogurt, and once I was done, I wandered into the living room. I was surprised to find Kendall standing looking out over the darkened city.

I walked over and put my hands on her arms, gently pulling her away from the window. "You okay?"

"I will be," she said, looking up at me.

"Can we talk?"

Our eyes locked and she nodded slightly as I guided her over to the couch. We both sat down and turned toward one another. I took in a deep breath, reached out, and took her hands into mine.

"What is it?" she questioned as I paused, unsure of where I should start.

"It's about the weekend," I began.

"Oh, Grayson, please, don't worry about it. It's done. It's over."

"No, it's not done."

"Sure it is. Grayson, please, we weren't together. What happened between us shouldn't have, but it did. Seriously, it's not a big deal."

"You're wrong. It matters. It matters to me. We should be together."

"Grayson, please..." Kendall took her hands from mine and stood up, walking back across the living room.

Instead of sitting there allowing her to walk away from me and continue spouting about how it didn't matter, I stood up and walked over to her, turning her toward me. "I want to be with you, Kendall."

She slowly lifted her eyes to mine and looked at me with shock. "You want to be with me? Grayson, I could never compare to the women you date."

"You're wrong. You are so much above the women I date it's not funny."

She was quiet for a moment, and she looked to the floor. "How am I supposed to know this will last?"

"You don't. No one does," I said, placing my finger on her chin and lifting her face to mine. "All I can say is that we do our best to make it work between us. What I can tell you is that, right now, I don't want to lose you, Kendall.

"Really?" she asked, tears lining her eyes.

"Really."

"I don't want to lose you either. I just don't want you doing this because you feel you have to."

I smiled softly. "You know, all these years, all those

girls, all I ever did was compare them to you. They couldn't hold a candle to you, and you know what?"

"What?"

"Out of them all, you are the only one who has lasted all these years. That has to speak for something."

I could tell she had no idea how to respond as she stood there looking into my eyes, tears flowing down her cheeks. I pulled her against me and finally relaxed as she wrapped her arms around me, burying her face into my chest.

"What do you say we give us a try?"

"I'd like that," she said, meeting my eyes.

I didn't wait any longer. I kissed her deeply, pulling her tight against me. "I think we should go crawl into bed," I said, kissing her again.

She didn't make me wait. Instead, she took me by the hand, pulled me down the hall, and shut the bedroom door behind us.

KENDALL

ONE YEAR LATER

I pulled a load of laundry from the dryer and carried the basket of unfolded clothes down to the bedroom, dumping them out on the bed. I pulled from the pile my two bathing suits and folded them, placing them in the suitcase. I figured this would be the last time this summer I'd be able to wear them. I wandered over to the closet and pulled out two of my favorite sundresses, folded those, and placed them on top the suitcase.

I glanced at the clock, closed the suitcase, and made my way into the washroom. Grayson would be home from the hospital any minute, and then we were heading up to Mom and Dad's cottage for the summer festival, only this year we were showing up as a real couple. I slipped out of my sweatpants and T-shirt and climbed in the shower, letting the hot water run over my body.

"Kendall, I'm home," I heard Grayson call from the bedroom.

"I'll be out in just a minute," I called from the shower, rinsing the last bit of the shampoo from my hair.

I felt a blast of cold air and turned around to see Grayson climbing into the shower. I smiled as he stepped closer and pulled me into his arms.

"I so love coming home and finding you in the shower," he whispered, and placed a kiss on the side of my neck. "I swear it's the most favorite part of my day."

"I love you finding me in here too." I giggled as he continued kissing my neck as his hands cupped my breasts.

"You know what else I love?"

"What?" I said, turning around in his arms.

"I love pushing you up against the wall, like this," he said as he placed his hands under my thighs, parting my legs and wrapping them around his waste as he pushed me against the wall.

I wrapped my arms around his neck and kissed his lips. "What time are we leaving?" he asked between kisses.

"I told Mom and Dad we'd be on our way by six," I said, kissing him again.

"Hate to break it to you, but we are going to be late."

"We are?"

"Hmm, yes, because I'm going to have my way with you before we get on the road."

I let out a laugh and then a deep moan as he sucked a nipple into his mouth and bit it gently.

"I CAN'T BELIEVE you guys are finally here," Jade said, looking at her watch as we walked through the door.

She wrapped her arms around me, hugging me tight. "Hey, Grayson," she said, moving to him.

"Hey, Jade, Rick," Grayson greeted.

"Here, let me help you get the stuff from the truck," Rick said, following Grayson out the door, each of them carrying in a suitcase and taking it down to the same basement bedroom we had shared the year prior.

The four of us made our way into the kitchen to find Mom and Dad both sitting at the table drinking tea.

"Hey, Grayson," Dad said, getting up and shaking his hand.

"Nice to see you again. How you feeling?" he questioned, taking on the familiar doctor tone I was used to hearing.

"Good, just had a follow up with Dr. Simpson. Everything checks out."

"Good to hear," Grayson said, sitting down beside me.

It had been exactly one year since we'd been here. A lot had happened in that year. After Dad's triple bypass, Grayson and I had finally gotten together. We'd spent the fall dating, and by Christmas, I had given my notice to my landlord and had moved in with him. We'd talked about getting married but had decided to wait until Grayson had finished his internship. Everything had fallen into place for us.

"Well, kids, I think we are going to head up to bed," Dad announced. "The festival starts early tomorrow, and we want to make sure we are there good and early to get a decent spot."

Dad and Mom both placed a kiss on my forehead before leaving, and I turned to see Jade smiling over at me. "Sure is different from last year," I said.

"Yeah, they decided to take a back seat to hosting their usual events this year. Dad really needs his rest more now," Jade said as we watched Mom and Dad climb the stairs up to their bedroom.

"What do you say we play a little truth or dare," Jade said, pulling out a tequila bottle from behind her.

I couldn't help but start laughing. "No, no way, not tonight."

"Oh come on. It could be a lot of fun now," she said, pressing the issue, but I stood my ground and shook my head.

"I think we are going to turn in too," Grayson said, taking hold of my hand. "I've had a long day."

"All right, guess we will see you guys in the morning," Jade said, taking hold of Rick's hand. "We could always go upstairs and have a little party on our own."

"All right, you two love birds, we'll see you in the morning."

I took Grayson's hand and followed him into the basement, entering the same room that our entire relationship started in. I closed the door behind us and turned to see Grayson standing looking at me. I walked over and stepped into his arms.

"Here we are," he whispered.

"Here we are," I repeated quietly as he rubbed the tip of his nose to mine.

He wrapped his arms around me and pulled me against him. "So, are you going to make me sleep on the floor this time?" he questioned.

"Not this time." I giggled.

"Thank God, because that floor is so hard, my back is still recovering." He laughed. "But are you sure you can trust me to behave?"

"Well, I'm never sure of that, but I'd like to think you can. After all, we are in my parents' house."

"That didn't stop me before, in case you forgot."

"No, I remember," I whispered, kissing him, undoing the button of his jeans.

"Whoa, whoa, who's misbehaving now."

I giggled as he pulled my fingers away. He grabbed our bag and threw it up on the bench that sat at the end of the bed. We quickly unpacked the bag, then got changed and crawled into bed.

Grayson climbed in, shut the light off, and then pulled

me against him, wrapping me tightly in his arms. I laid there and listened to the steady sound of his breathing, my head spinning with the news I'd found out earlier today. I had no idea how I was going to tell him and figured there was probably no better time than now.

"Grayson, you awake," I whispered.

"Mmmm."

"Grayson. Are you awake?"

"Sweetie, I was just about asleep. What is it?"

"I need to tell you something."

"Okay."

"Ahm, you remember not too long ago when I thought I had the flu."

"Yeah."

"It wasn't the flu. I was at the doctor today."

"What is it? What's wrong?" he asked, reaching up and turning the light on. He looked down at me, a serious look resting on his face. "Is it serious?"

I smiled at him and placed my finger on his lips, signaling for him to stop speaking. "Shhh, it's not life-threatening."

"So what did he do, pop you on a mild antibiotic?" he asked, lying back down and placing his arm behind his head. "Cause I know you haven't been feeling the greatest lately, even though you keep trying to hide it from me."

"Not exactly."

"Well, what then?" he asked, getting slightly irritated.

"Remember how we were thinking of getting a slightly bigger place so you could have an office?"

"Yeah."

"I think it might be time to do that."

"Why? I told you the spare room, even though it's cramped, will do just fine for now. I was able to fit the desk in that little spot behind the boxes."

"It won't."

"Sure it will. I'll make due. I just need a place to be able to sit and do reports."

"I know, but in about eight months, there will be a crib in place of your desk."

Grayson was quiet, and I seriously worried that he was in some sort of shock. I sat up and looked down at him as he stared into my eyes.

"Are you serious?" he asked, a smile coming to his lips.

I nodded. "Yes. The blood work came back today. The office called me this afternoon."

He wrapped me in his arms tight, hugging me.

"Are you happy?"

"Happy? Are you crazy. I am ecstatic. I just can't believe you didn't tell me earlier."

"I wasn't going to tell you this weekend at all, but then I couldn't figure out how I was going to come up with an excuse not to drink." I giggled.

Grayson kicked the covers back and got up out of bed, turned the light on, and started sifting through his bag.

"What are you doing?" I questioned.

"I was going to wait until the end of the festival, maybe even the end of the summer to do this, but now is as good a time as any," he said, still digging through his bag.

"For what?" I questioned.

"This," he said, coming around my side of the bed and holding out his hand to produce a black velvet box.

"What is this?" I asked, looking from him to his hand and back to him.

He didn't say anything. He just opened the box to produce a beautiful white-gold engagement ring. "Kendall, will you marry me?" he asked quietly.

I covered my mouth with my hands and nodded. "Oh, my God, yes." I crashed into him, hugging him tightly.

"I wanted this to be way more romantic," he said, chuckling as I held him tighter.

"More romantic? It's perfect," I said, kissing his lips.

ABOUT THE ALL AMERICAN BOYS SERIES

I hope you enjoyed my book, The Boy Under the Gazebo, which is part of the shared world of the All American Boys Series.

Would you like to read all of them? Find them here on Kindle Unlimited.

Welcome to Bear Creek, Colorado, an idyllic all-American mountain resort town and home of the USA Music Festival. Filled with summer love, country music and unexpected pleasures, this brand new series of short contemporary stories will bring together a mix of summer fun and music with the backdrop of the Colorado Rocky Mountains.

The Boyfriend Pact by Emily Robertson
Boy Business by Megan Matthews
Boy, I'm Yours by Molly McLain

The Boy Upstairs by Amanda Shelley
Oh Boy! By Hope Irving
A Boy and His Dog by Chloe Holiday
Boyfriend Material by Marie Ahls
The Boyfriend Checklist by Sierra Hill
The Boy I Shouldn't Want by Stephanie Rose
The Boy I Can't Forget by S. Moose
The Boy Under the Gazebo by S.L. Sterling
The Boy I Loved by Leanne Davis
Inked Boy by C.A. Harms
Boy and the Family Plan by Anna Hague
Small Town Boy by K.L. Humphreys

A NOTE FROM THE AUTHOR

Dear Readers,

I would like to thank you for taking the time to read *The Boy Under the Gazebo part of the All-American Boys Series. I loved writing this story and I hope that you enjoyed Kendall and Grayson's story as much as I did.* If you did, I would love it if you would drop me a review. Reviews are so important and really help me; plus I love to hear what my readers think.

Coming Soon

Doctor Desire (Doctors of Eastport General) March 4, 2022

Ace (Book 2 Vegas MMA) Release Date 2022

Blade (Book 3 Vegas MMA) Release Date 2022

ABOUT S.L. STERLING

S.L. Sterling had been an avid reader since she was a child, often found getting lost in books. Today if she isn't writing or plotting, she can be found buried in a romance novel. S.L. Sterling lives with her husband and dog in Northern Ontario.

Stay up to date by signing up for my Newsletter

Visit my Website

Join my Street Team
Sterlings Silver Sapphires

OTHER TITLES BY S.L. STERLING

It Was Always You

On A Silent Night

Bad Company

Back to You this Christmas

Fireside Love

Holiday Wishes

All American Boys Series

Saviour Boy

The Malone Brother Series

A Kiss Beneath the Stars

In Your Arms

His to Hold

Finding Forever with You

Vegas MMA

Dagger

All I Want for Christmas (Contemporary Romance Holiday
Collection)

Constraint (KB Worlds: Everyday Heroes)

CPSIA information can be obtained
at www.ICGtesting.com
Printed in the USA
LVHW111731261021
701609LV00004B/194